T0356441

THE BLACK CURTAIN

CORNELL WOOLRICH (1903–1968) is the pen name most often employed by one of America's best crime and noir writers, whose other pseudonyms included George Hopley and William Irish. His novels were among the first to employ the atmosphere, outlook, and impending sense of doom that came to be characterized as noir, and inspired some of the most famous films of the period, including Alfred Hitchcock's *Rear Window*, Francois Truffaut's *The Bride Wore Black*, *The Phantom Lady*, and celebrated B-movies such as *The Leopard Man* and *Black Angel*.

GEORGE PELECANOS is the author of twenty two novels and story collections set in and around Washington, DC, and has been the recipient of numerous international writing awards. He is a screenwriter, essayist, and television writer/producer whose credits include *The Wire*, *Treme*, *The Deuce*, and *We Own This City*. He lives in Silver Spring, Maryland.

THE BLACK CURTAIN

CORNELL WOOLRICH

Introduction by
GEORGE PELECANOS

AMERICAN MYSTERY CLASSICS

Penzler Publishers
New York

Published in 2025 by Penzler Publishers
58 Warren Street, New York, NY 10007
penzlerpublishers.com

Distributed by W. W. Norton

Cover image: Andy Ross
Cover design: Mauricio Diaz

Paperback ISBN 978-1-61316-628-4
Hardcover ISBN 978-1-61316-627-7

Library of Congress Control Number: 2024945200

Printed in the United States of America

9 8 7 6 5 4 3 2 1

INTRODUCTION

CORNELL WOOLRICH was a worker. He produced a large amount on the printed page in a relatively short window of time. He wrote, by my count, twenty-seven novels and countless short stories in various genres, which were later compiled in numerous collections. The books and stories were a natural source for the movies, as their plots neatly fit the mold of three-act screenwriting: conflict, deeper conflict, and resolution. There were forty-three (!) feature films made from his books and short stories, which ultimately made him a very wealthy man, an unusual outcome for a writer who toiled in the pulps.

The most famous of the films mined from the Woolrich library is probably, and deservedly, Hitchcock's *Rear Window* (1954), adapted from the Woolrich short story "It Had to Be Murder." There were other very good ones: *The Leopard Man* (directed by Jacques Tourneur, 1943); *The Chase* (directed by Arthur Ripley, 1946); the underrated *I Wouldn't Be in Your Shoes* (directed by William Nigh, 1948); and *The Window* (directed by Ted Tetzlaff, 1949).

Street of Chance (1942), a passable picture directed by Jack Hively and starring Burgess Meredith and noir mainstay Clair

Trevor, was adapted from *The Black Curtain*, the book you hold in your hands. There were Woolrich-inspired films by Indian and Japanese directors, and one from Italian Giallo/horror/Euro-crime practitioner Umberto Lenzi (*Seven Blood-Stained Orchids*, 1972). Rainer Werner Fassbinder directed *Martha* (1974); Francois Truffaut directed *The Bride Wore Black* (1968) and *Mississippi Mermaid* (1969). For a Hitchcock acolyte, Truffaut made surprisingly dull suspense films, but it should be noted, if it's to your taste, that *The Bride Wore Black*'s premise inspired Quentin Tarentino's *Kill Bill*. My favorite Woolrich movie adaptation is Robert Siodmak's *Phantom Lady* (1944), a delirious high-water mark of film noir.

What of the books?

Woolrich started his writing career with Fitgerald-inspired, Jazz Age novels that were sold in numbers and well received. This sent him out to Hollywood for a shot at screenwriting. The Depression ended the market for Roaring Twenties lit and Woolrich turned to mystery/suspense fiction. He was prolific from 1940–1960, so prolific that he was compelled to publish under other names (my hardback edition of *Phantom Lady*, under Collier's Front Page Mysteries imprint, carries the pseudonym William Irish on its spine). *The Black Curtain* was the second of Woolrich's six novels with "Black" in the title, which is a tipoff to the darkness of the work.

Can Woolrich be described as a noir novelist? He was among them, though I don't think he (or anyone else) invented the form. Noir rose up simultaneously, perhaps unconsciously, amongst other arts. It's there in German Expressionist films and design, it's in Edward Hopper paintings, in jazz music (through association), in literature. Though Boris Ingster's *The Stranger on the Third Floor* (1940) is usually credited as the first film noir, mainly because of its expressionistic nightmare sequence, I'd put Fritz

Lang's *M* (1931) in the running as well. The point being, there were no "firsts" in noir.

The Black Curtain was published in 1941, before anyone knew what noir "was" (it took the French to put a label on it, years later). Yet, deliberate or not, Woolrich wrote in a style that was very precise in conveying anxiety, fear, claustrophobia, and the inevitability of fate, elements that were to become the emotional core of the genre and would be conveyed by film directors with visual style in a distinct blend of lighting and effects. In Woolrich's later books, there is evidence that he was being influenced by the visual signposts of film noir (venetian blind shadows, etc.), but at this stage in his career, perhaps inadvertently, he was creating something new. Even as early as *The Black Curtain*, he equated fractured illumination with impending violence, as in the "blades of light" that divided a space or the way light "knifed" its way into a room.

From *The Black Curtain*:

Townsend stood there by the tree, watching her down the leafy alley. Now the disks of sunlight didn't gently alternate down on her; they streaked in one continuous, blurred line like a striped tiger pelt, she was running so fast.

At times in *The Black Curtain*, one can sense that Woolrich was writing in a fever, manifested in his staccato prose. The rhythm maintains the anxiety and works to great effect:

The door seemed to explode with impacts. It made the light bulbs jitter in the ceiling. It made a pottery thing on a table sing out with the vibration, carried to it along the floor and up the table legs. It was an earthquake of an attempted forcible entry. It was violence in its most ravening form. It was the night gone hydrophobic at their threshold. It was disaster. It was the end.

Much has been made of Woolrich's tortured life and how it spills onto the pages, like blood from a freshly opened wound, of his work. There are some facts backed up by interviews of his friends and editors: He was an odd-looking man, pale and small. He had one brief marriage that fell apart and thereafter lived in low-grade residences with his mother in New York City. He rarely left his apartments and was probably agoraphobic (fear of the marketplace, from the Greek). He suffered from thanatophobia (fear of death, from the Greek, just saying). He was an alcoholic. When his mother passed away, his life spiraled downward and his health rapidly declined. Towards the end, one of his legs was amputated due to gangrene left unattended. He died with nearly a million dollars in the bank (from the movie money, a fortune in 1968), which he willed to Columbia University for a scholarship fund for writing students in honor of his mother. Did any of these things make their way into his fiction? Probably, in the same way that a writer's psyche *always* makes its way into the fiction.

As for his rumored queer life and his infamous sailor suit, much as been made of it, and I'm not sure why. It's never been proven, nor has it been confirmed that his marriage was never consummated. His private life was his, and for me it has no relevance to his work.

I'm content to read the books and not overanalyze the man behind them. Woolrich's output was, frankly, uneven. But when the author was creatively locked in, his books and short stories were terrific. *The Black Curtain* is a crackling good mystery/suspense novel. I'm pleased to own this new edition for my collection. I think you will be, too.

GEORGE PELECANOS
Silver Spring, MD
May 2024

THE BLACK
CURTAIN

BOOK I
The Curtain

1

FIRST EVERYTHING was blurred. Then he could feel hands fumbling around him, lots of hands. They weren't actually touching him; they were touching things that touched him. He got their feel one step removed. Flinging away small, loose objects like chunks of mortar or fragments of brick, which seemed to be strewn all over him. Every minute there was less of these.

Then, dimly, he heard a voice say: "Here's the ambulance now." Another answered: "Bring him over here, where they can get at him easier."

He felt himself being moved, set down again. He tried to open his eyes, and a lot of grit and dust settled into them, stung them shut again the first time. The second time he tried it he was able to make it. He got a blinding flash of light-blue sky. Faces were peering down at him, upside down, around the perimeter of it.

He could feel his coat and shirt being spread open and then pressure being applied along his sides. "No ribs broken." Someone flexed his arms and then his legs. "No broken bones anywhere. He got off easy. Just that nasty bump on his head."

He was righted to a sitting position, and a trickle of plaster or something spilled down off his hair. The intern said: "O.K., brother, we'll dress it up, and that ought to take care of it for you."

He dabbed something on it that burned and made the man jump. Then he plastered something over it. "All right, I guess you can stand up now."

They helped him to his feet; he reached out and steadied himself against one of them first. Then he was able to stay up by himself.

"You want to take a ride in with us, anyway, and have yourself checked over?" the intern asked, closing up his case.

"No, I'm all right," he said. He wanted to get home. It must be late. Virginia would be waiting for him. He didn't like to be late.

"O.K., but if you don't feel good, you better come around and have yourself looked at."

"Yeah," he said, "I will."

A cop shoved forward with poised notebook and said, "Let me have your name and address."

"Frank Townsend," he said unhesitatingly. "Eight-twenty Rutherford Street, North."

That was all. The ambulance had already clanged off. The cop turned away, finishing up his report as he went. A smear of rubble on the sidewalk and a jagged rent in the roof coping of the building immediately beside it were the only remaining signs of what had just happened. The thick cluster of onlookers grouped about began to fan out and disperse. Townsend turned and began to worm his way out through them.

A youngster of twelve or so called after him: "Hey, here's your hat! I picked it up for you."

Townsend turned and took it from him, dusted it off sketchily, reversed it to put it on. Then he stood still, staring down inside it. It had "D N" initialed on the sweatband.

He shook his head to the kid, tried to return it. "Where'd you get it? This isn't mine—"

"Sure it's yours! I seen it roll off you when you went down!"

Townsend cast his eyes doubtfully over the littered sidewalk and the gutter alongside, but there was no other hat in sight.

The kid was eying him askance. "Don't you know your own hat, mister?"

Some of the grownups laughed. They were all standing around, gaping at him. He wanted to get away. He was still shaky, from the accident. He wanted to get home. He tried the hat on and it fit his head to a T. It had that telltale feeling of having been on a hundred times before.

He left it on and made his way up the street, but he knew that he was wearing somebody else's initials on his head.

He looked around him, and he couldn't understand what he was doing around here, what had brought him here in the first place. It was a slum street, swarming with humanity, and riddled with pushcarts. Some mission from the office? Some errand from Virginia? Whatever it was, the shock of the accident had knocked it completely out of his mind. He turned the corner, passing under a street sign that read "Tillary Street," and, once around it, reached absently into his pocket for a cigarette while he continued on his homeward way.

Instead of the familiar cheap, crumpled pack he was used to carrying around him for days at a time until it practically shredded to pieces, he brought up a sleek enamel case, wafer thin, banded in gold, flashing at him with malignant brilliance.

He dropped it as though it had bitten him. He stared at it where it lay for long minutes. Then finally he stooped, picked it up with an unsteady hand, opened and examined it. Its fill wasn't even his own brand. There was no inscription inside or out, nothing to show whose it was or where he'd got it.

He put it back in his pocket and forced himself to go on. He was afraid to stand there too long and let himself think about it too much. A strange terror darted in and out of the air just over his head, and he was afraid to attract it full force, as one is of lightning. He wanted to get home, now, more than ever.

He had to board a bus, he was so far out of the way. He rode all the way up in it in a sort of shadow, though it was well lighted inside.

He got off, turned a corner, and the familiar reaches of Rutherford Street opened before his gaze at last. He trudged down it toward his flat. Just a few doors more now and he'd be in. Familiar as the street was, there was something a little different about it. Details seemed to have altered here and there, but he couldn't tell just which ones they were. He saw the same familiar kids playing around; they all looked bigger to him.

He sighted his house just ahead, and when he had reached it and turned to go in, he stopped suddenly, stood rigid, his foot on the bottommost entrance step. His face froze, looking over at his own two ground-floor windows, on the left. What had happened since this morning? What in God's name had taken place?

The curtains were gone from the windows. The panes were cloudy, filmed with dust, as though they hadn't been washed in weeks. Virginia always kept the windows sparkling, crystalline. How could they have got into such a state since just this morning? She must have taken ashes or scouring powder and blurred them on purpose; maybe this was some new cleansing method she was trying out. She'd taken her potted geranium off the sill, too.

He went in, still pale, palpitating from the shock his nervous system had just received. He found he'd lost his key, probably at the scene of the accident. He didn't waste time looking for it; he wanted to get inside, away from all this strangeness. He knocked, rattled the knob hectically.

She didn't come to the door. She didn't let him in. He couldn't stand still. He went back to the entrance and rang for Mrs. Fromm, the janitor's wife.

She came right up. She showed an inordinate amount of surprise at sight of him. So she was going to be part of the strangeness, too. "Mr. Townsend! Well what are *you* doing around here?"

"What am I—?" he repeated dazedly.

"You thinking of taking your old flat back? Just say the word. It's here waiting, the last tenants only moved out six weeks ago."

"My old flat? Six weeks—" He put his hand to the wall, to steady himself. "Could I have a drink of water, please?"

She ran to get it for him, alarmed.

He could feel his hackles rise, as in the presence of some chilling, unfathomable mystery. He tried to get a tight grip on his mental equilibrium, keep it level at all costs. "I'm Frank Townsend. I've come home like I do every day from work. Why should this happen to me?"

By the time she had come back, he had forced himself into a glazed semblance of calm. Instinctively, he knew that neither Mrs. Fromm nor any other outsider could help him in this. He would only get involved in all sorts of delays, maybe even be hauled off into confinement. There was only one person to go to, there was only one person he could fully trust. He wanted to get quickly to his Virginia, wherever she was. But where was she?

He said, trying to sound casual, "Could you tell me where I can find my wife? Some falling plaster hit me on the head just now, and I guess I'm a little dizzy, came here by mistake—"

She paled, but she gave him what he was hoping for. "Your wife's living around on Anderson Avenue now, Mr. Townsend, two blocks down, the second house from the corner. She stopped in here several times to see if there was any mail for her, that's how I happen to know."

"Thanks," he said expiringly, backing away. "Isn't it funny how I—uh—got balled up?"

She followed him to the street entrance, shaking her head concernedly. "I wouldn't neglect a thing like that if I were you, you may have a slight concussion—"

He turned and walked away rapidly, his heart going like a trip hammer. He was more than just frightened now. The terrifying mysteries mounted. First, initials on his hatband that didn't match his name. Then a cigarette case that he'd never seen before, filled with a brand that he'd never smoked before, in his pocket. Now an empty flat when he got home; his abode changed, without warning, between morning and evening. And yet the janitress speaking as though it had been weeks or months. He began to run toward Anderson Avenue.

He found the place at last, and it was with a feeling close to horror that he sighted a name, her name and yet not hers, on one of the letter boxes when he scanned them: "Miss Virginia Morrison." What was she doing over here in this strange house, under her maiden name? Why had she left the other one so quickly? What had taken place there?

Whatever this whole thing was that had happened, he knew

he was about to have it explained to him. In just a few minutes now. And that was no solace. For it had plunged to depths of strangeness that no ordinary explanation would reach any more. He almost dreaded explanation as much as he did continuing mystification now.

He rang the bell, and the door catch was released for him. He went inside into the inner hallway and to the door that bore a matching number to the one on the bell. He stopped before it and waited.

Minutes passed that no one's life should hold. Minutes of deliriumlike strangeness, in which nothing happened, minutes tense with waiting for something to happen, and wondering what it would be.

He heard steps approaching on the other side of the door, and he shrank back a little, away from them, on the side on which he was. Then the knob turned, and the latch tongue drew in, and the door opened a little—to face-width—and there they were, looking at each other.

He and she. Frank Townsend and his wife Virginia.

He'd called her his rag doll. She always reminded him of a rag doll. One of the pert kind, that sits all contorted on the edge of a dresser. Maybe because she was long-limbed and had a way of flinging herself about in chairs. Not just dropping into them rearwards, but going into them sidewards, over their arms. Then, too, she had a way of wearing her hair cut in a straight line above her eyes. That helped. And her mouth was very small, like a red-outlined pucker half the time. That was her.

But now—the rag doll was all limp and wilted. And though she hadn't changed, yet she had changed. Everything was the same, and yet everything was not quite the same. Just a little faded, just a little toned down, not quite as shiny.

He thought she was going to fall out on the floor at his feet. But her grip on the door held her. She leaned her forehead against the door frame for a minute, as though her eyes were very tired and she wanted to rest them in that way, by supporting her entire head.

Then suddenly she was against him, in his arms.

She kept breathing against him as though she couldn't get enough air. He couldn't breathe very well himself; it was sort of catching.

"Virginia, honey, let me come in," he said. "I'm frightened. Queer things have been happening. I want to be inside with you."

She closed the door with her back, holding him with both hands, as if the door were an active agency that might siphon him out again if she didn't hang on to him. Then he was in the bedroom, sitting on the edge of one of their familiar twin beds, taking off his shoes. One bed, he noticed, had been stripped down; even the mattress had been removed from it. Its bare frame had been shunted aside against the wall, and an accumulation of boxes and other nondescript paraphernalia littered it. The other was in perfect order. He lay back on it and she came in with a cold compress and put it on his head.

Then she sat down beside him, held his hand between both of hers, and pressed it to her cheek. She didn't say anything. He could tell she was afraid, just as he was.

He kept staring at her questioningly. Finally he blurted out: "Virginia, that bottle of rye someone gave me for Christmas—"

"I've still got it," she said in a choked voice. She got up and went out. He had a feeling he was going to need it.

She came back and handed him a glass. He held it clutched tightly, as though his very life might depend in having it within reach. "Virginia, I feel funny. I'm like lost. I don't understand. Maybe it's only that clout on the head. But I've got to hear it from you. There were a couple of little things on the street already, but they don't matter, I'll let them go. The main thing is: what made you do it? What made you move so suddenly without telling me? Why, when I left this morning to go to work—"

Her hands flew to her mouth, latticing it with rigid intercrossed fingers. A choked cry forced its way through them.

He reared up toward her, on the bed. He pulled the impediment of her hands down by main force. "Virginia, speak to me!"

"Frank, oh my God, what are you saying? *This morning*—? I moved to this apartment from Rutherford Street over a year and a half ago!"

They were two very sick and frightened people. His wrist made a quick hitch and he gulped the bracer of whisky. The glass rocked empty on the bed beside him. He held his skull tightly pressed with both hands, as if to keep it from flying apart.

"I can remember kissing you good-by at the door!" he said helplessly. "I can remember you calling out after me to remind me, 'Sure you've got your muffler? It's cold out.'"

"Frank," she said. "The weather alone should tell you—it's warm out, you're not wearing a muffler or even a coat now. You left me in the winter, and now it's spring. You left me on January thirtieth, 1938. I never forgot that date, how could I? And today is—Wait, I'll let you read it for yourself."

She staggered out of the room once more, came back with a newspaper, that evening's newspaper, handed it to him.

He scanned the date line feverishly. "May 10, 1941."

Then he dropped it and its loosened sheets cascaded all over the floor, and he was digging the heels of his hands desperately under the bony ridges of his eye sockets. "My God! What happened to all that *time*? Those weeks, those months, those years—I can remember everything so perfectly, every last detail, up to that morning. I can remember what we had for breakfast. I can even remember we went to the movies the night before, to see MacDonald and Eddy in *Rosalie*. It seems like *last* night. And just now, the molding of a building fell on me, on Tillary Street, and when they'd helped me up, I simply kept on coming home, to where I belonged. But what happened to those years between?"

"Don't you remember anything at all?"

"They're gone like the tick of a second. Less than that, for even the tick of a single second can remain in your memory if you try hard enough. They're gone as though they never were."

"Maybe if we get a doctor—"

"No doctor can bring them back. They happened to *me*, not to him."

"I've read about cases like this before," she tried to reassure him. "Amnesia, I think they call it. Somewhere between home and your work after you left me that last morning, something must have happened to you, some accident, some blow, just like what happened to you tonight on Tillary Street. Maybe a wild baseball thrown by some boys hit you on the head. Whatever it was, you picked yourself up, outwardly unhurt—and you didn't know who you were any more, forgot where you were going, forgot to come back home to me. And none of the people around you, that saw it happen, were any the wiser. Your suit had just come back from the cleaner's that morning. You left in kind of a hurry, without taking time to transfer most of the personal trifles you usually carried around in your pockets from the old one to the new one. Any one of them—an address on an old envelope, a receipted bill—would have helped you. But without them you were cut off completely."

Then, presently, she said, "Frank, you're back now. That's all that counts. Let's forget about it."

He felt less starkly frightened, as the hours wore on and they talked it over. Deep down within him he was still greatly troubled, far more troubled than she. That was natural. It was his identity that had been lost, not hers. She had him back, for her the mystery was solved. For him it was still impenetrable, yawning behind him like an abyss seen from a safely regained, sunlit ledge. One misstep, and—

In the still of that night, long after they'd put out the lights and lay quiet in the darkened room, he suddenly started upright, cold sweat needling his forehead. "Virginia, I'm scared! Put on the lights, I'm frightened of the dark! Where was I? *Who* was I, all that time?"

2

He had his old job back. Or at least, another with the same employers. In the weeks immediately following his disappearance, she had told them, in answer to their repeated inquiries, that he had suffered a nervous breakdown, had had to go away for a rest. Pride had made her do that. She couldn't bear to have anyone think she didn't know where he was, what had become of him. So now, when he had presented himself down there once more, room had been made for him with the fewest possible questions asked, and those wholly of a sympathetic nature. That had made it much less embarrassing.

The old familiar routine was beginning to reclaim his daily life. The blank was beginning to recede more and more into the past. He was even daring to hope that perhaps, at some not too future date, it would become one of those dimly remembered, never-mentioned things that two people share in common but never speak about.

The days were growing longer, and he emerged onto a street still bright with setting sunlight as he left his place of work. He bought a paper at the corner stand to take home with him, then hurried to his usual place for boarding the bus, joining the one or two others who were already standing there.

He spread his paper and began scanning it while he was waiting there. Held that way, it shielded the lower part of his face, although he wasn't thinking of that.

He had been standing there perhaps two minutes—the bus was evidently a little behind schedule—when something made his eyelids twitch and he raised them. It was that feeling of being looked at intently.

There was a man about to pass him in the crowd streaming along the sidewalk. Townsend's suddenly revealed face had caught his vacant attention just as it peered over the paper. The roving glance became a fixed stare. The fixed stare became a searching scrutiny.

The starer broke his headlong stride. He took a shorter step. He forgot to take the next one altogether, held his foot poised toe to ground. He had faltered almost to a full stop by now.

The lens of Townsend's mind snapped, developed, and printed him—all in one instantaneous process. He was sturdily built, a little below medium height but not short. The brim of his hat cut off his hair—except at the sides, where it was sheared too close to show any distinctive color—but his eyes were gray and agatelike under thick, dark brows. Hard eyes, seldom softened. The kind that don't laugh. It was hard to tell who or what he was just by looking at him. He could have been anything. He was a face in the crowd, and Townsend didn't know him, had never seen him before in his life.

But the face didn't go on; held back, like a white rock peering steadily through rippling, coursing water. Something made an alarm bell of danger start ringing in Townsend's heart. People don't stop and scan you exhaustively on the street for no reason. This man recognized him or thought he recognized him but wasn't altogether sure yet. Whatever it was, there was no innocent social acquaintanceship at the root of it. The man's own actions showed that. Still uncertain in his own mind, he realized belatedly that he was attracting attention to himself, putting Townsend on his guard, by staring so overtly. He tried to undo the damage by continuing on his way—rather too abruptly for it to be plausible—and seeming to recede into the distance along the bustling sidewalk, in the direction he had originally been following.

But not for very far. Some show-window display not far ahead seemed to attract his interest, and he veered inward toward it, on a long diagonal—that began a considerable distance before he could possibly have seen just what it was he was being drawn to with any degree of accuracy. He came to a halt before it, back to sidewalk and peered absorbedly in. Show windows make good reflecting surfaces, Townsend knew.

The alarm bell within was a din by now. "I'm going to get out of here!" he assured himself grimly.

He kept his head inscrutably motionless while he weighed possibilities. The bus would be simply a four-wheeled trap, if this unknown chose to follow him aboard. Once the two of them were inside it, he'd never be able to get out again undetected.

If he returned inside his own place of work and waited a few minutes for a later bus, the stalker might still be lurking around when he came out again—and he would then know where Townsend came from every day at this hour, which he didn't as yet.

If he simply took a walk around the block, in hopes of throwing him off, and then came back here to his original starting point—well, two could walk around the block as well as one, at a spaced distance.

The hunted or troubled thing, whether two legged or four, instinctively seeks a hole in the ground. There is no cover like a hole in the ground. The next street over there was a subway. He'd never used it before, because it diverged a great deal further than just one street at the other end, where his destination was. It was not the straightest line between here and his home.

But some action was better than the threat latent in this veiled surveillance and the acute uneasiness it was instilling in him. He decided to try to gain the subway, if it could be managed.

He edged the tip of his nose around a little, without staring over his shoulder full face. That show case was holding the stranger a long time, back there. Too long a time. Townsend, who worked in the immediate vicinity, knew which one it was. It was a shop displaying surgical belts and trusses. Whatever else he lacked, the window shopper didn't need any corrective aids for posture. His back was ruler straight and his waist was spare and flexible.

Townsend readied himself by surreptitiously telescoping his newspaper's width. He waited for the light to change, and then he made a break for it. Didn't burgeon into full flight, but started off at a brisk, unexpected walk.

He didn't look back while he was still in the open, crossing over between pavements. He felt an awful compulsion, the instinct of all stalked things, but he kept himself from it. He gained the opposite curb, and the corner building line knifed across their mutual line of vision, severing it momentarily.

Instantly his brisk walk changed to a long, loping run, that ate up ground without being harried enough to arouse suspicion in the passers-by.

The crosswise street wasn't long; in fact wasn't long enough to gain him a proper head start. But ahead a clean-cut, oblong gap, like a trap in the ground, was his goal. He gained it. His heels ticked off the steel-rimmed steps, with a sound a little bit like dice being shaken. It *was* a chance; he had no choice but to take it.

Then, halfway down the steps, he stopped and looked back the way he had come, eyes on a level with people's shoes. What he saw sent him hurtling the rest of the way down.

The man was careening up the street after him full tilt. He meant business; he meant to hang onto Townsend at all costs.

Townsend, station level gained, had a choice: of crossing below ground to the matching stairs on the opposite side and scampering up them to the street again—in which case the chase would simply be resumed on the opposite sidewalk—or of taking refuge out on the platform. A wait of even a single minute for a train would maroon him, leave him helpless.

A surging roar, like a high wind caught in the tunnel, punctuated with a green eye and a red one, decided him. It might take more than a minute to clear the station again, but he might be able to lose himself in the crowd aboard. He dove for a turnstile just as the track orifice exploded into a razzle-dazzle of illuminated car windows, streaming the length of the platform apron.

He blessed the meticulousness of habit that always made him have a nickel ready at hand, separate from the rest of his change in a pocket of its own, to use as carfare on his way to or from work. It saved, at all times, precious seconds of winnowing through pennies, dimes, and quarters. It averted, now, the catastrophe of having to detour to the change booth, of being almost certainly overtaken while filing by it. The lighted mirror in the receptacle magnified the head of Thomas Jefferson to an ugly death mask, and he cracked through.

Seconds were going to decide the outcome, he knew, but he'd made the gamble and he couldn't back out now. He avoided the nearest car opening as being too obvious a refuge, sprinted for one far down the line, out of sight of the steps, gauging to a nicety how much time he had before they were sealed up again. He reached the third car down as the doors were starting to slide closed. He sandwiched himself in sidewise, just quickly enough to avoid contact with the door, which would have meant thrusting back the rubber-insulated door edge and delaying the whole process of closing up the train, from car to car.

He'd won. Or had he? The tiny illuminated, red door indicators went out. The control signal was relayed to the motorman. The train was effectively walled off from the station, before it had even moved an inch. But if the pursuer had had sense enough to plunge for the nearest car opening, the one Townsend had avoided, he might have made it, he might be somewhere on the jammed train at this very moment.

Townsend had a sick feeling at the thought, and let his shoulders sag down a little in the corner formed by the two sides of the vestibule that supported him. The cars started to glide forward, the platform to drop behind.

He was spared the added agony of uncertainty, all the long way home, of not knowing from one moment to the next when he might feel the sudden clutch of a heavy, restraining hand falling on him from out the anonymous crowd or of being discovered and kept steadily in view without his knowing it by agate-hard eyes under a shading hat brim, to be followed off the train at his destination and overtaken in more favorable, isolated surroundings.

As his own car gained the mid-point of the platform, he saw his pursuer on it, still outside the train. Something must have gone wrong with his timing. Any one of countless things could have thwarted him. Maybe he hadn't had the right coin ready—if indeed he had bothered inserting one at all, and not just ducked below the turnstile arm, as seemed more likely. Maybe he'd had too many possibilities to cover at once—the platform, the station washroom, concealment behind one of the weight machines—and the momentary hesitation had cost him his chance. Or, most likely of all, maybe the outgoing surge of passengers on the stairs, which Townsend had been just in time enough to avoid, had balked his getting down them until it was too late. Townsend had won the gamble.

He was running along, pacing the train but falling steadily behind it, peering hawklike in through the lighted windows one by one as they outdistanced him. Townsend's vestibule door pane caught up with him and their stares met eye to eye, for the second and last time that day. Terror, still unassuaged by safety, meeting with some grim inflexible purpose.

He didn't try to dissemble any more, the man outside the bleared glass. He'd lost Townsend that way the first time. He didn't try to pretend he had no purpose, or that his purpose was anything but Townsend. Without a change shadowing his frozen expression, without a flicker of emotion lighting his cold-gray eyes, he deliberately reached backhand to his hip and drew a gun.

Townsend was too paralyzed with horror at the incredible action to be able even to drop below the shelter of the steel lower half of the door. Knee joints often weaken with terror; his had become locked, unmanageable. He was as rigid as a bird fascinated by a snake. He was too wedged in by the oblivious people around him to have been able to move much in any direction.

He didn't fire in at him, as Townsend had first thought for a crazed moment he intended to. He swung his arm up overhead and slashed at the door panel with the gun heft. It cracked with a dull thud, white veins streaked through it, and it sagged inward in a small, cone-shaped blister, almost as though it were malleable. But it held, none of the pieces fell out.

He was trying to break the pane, to reach in through the opening from where he was, snag the overhead emergency cord, and bring the train to a stop. Maniacal, but not a physical impossibility, provided he balanced a foot on the tiny lip of the car base, clutched one of the outside, between-car hand grips made use of by the conductors themselves, and let the moving train carry him for the remaining moment or two before the tunnel wall nudged him off. He would have been taking a gamble of his own, on being able to bring the train to a stop before he was drawn into the tunnel shaft with it and crushed to death.

Outside forces interfered to prevent him. The serge-sleeved arms of a station guard suddenly twined about him from behind, grappled with him, pulled him up short—and clear. The Laocoönlike formation whisked from sight, left behind. The lighted platform snuffed out, became black tunnel wall. The train sped on unimpeded.

The thought Townsend took with him the rest of the way home was: "He could have shot me. He seemed to want me alive." It had no power to relieve his terror.

He didn't tell Virginia any of it. What was there he could tell her? Only draw terrifying shadow outlines, without being able to fill in their meaning. A stranger on a street had pursued him.

That was either too much or too little. He didn't know who the man was, nor what he wanted with him, nor even who it was that *he*, the one wanted, was supposed to be.

He only knew that the bottomless black abyss of that anonymous past was not passive, lifeless, after all; it had just emitted a blood-red lick of flame toward him, as if seeking to drag him back into its depths and consume him.

3

A DAY went by, holding its breath; then another, beginning to breathe more easily. Then, on the third, the wind was knocked out of his confidence again. He saw it once more, the Face in the Crowd.

An accident saved him. Less than an accident; perhaps the most trivial thing there is that can make a walker stop. On his way out of the building where he worked he stopped. He tripped over a loosened shoelace. He saw Agate Eyes go by outside, at that moment, the man who had hounded him to the subway. They were only feet away from each other, closer even than they had been three days before. Their elbows brushed, metaphorically speaking. The man crossed the width of the arched opening, passed from view on the sidewalk. But for the errant shoelace Townsend would have emerged just in time to cut across his path, practically tread on his toes.

He knew he wasn't mistaken, it was the man. He was already as familiar to Townsend as a bad dream—he had been in so many of them with him the past few nights—the bulky shoulders, the spare waist, his swing when he walked, that comes from perfect muscular co-ordination. He'd had on the same clothes and the same hat, and he'd been wearing the same eyes too, cold and hard and gray.

Townsend's first impulse was to turn and plunge back into the depths of the building, put the length of the arcade between himself and this omnipresent menace.

Instead, he found himself being irresistibly drawn forward to peer out after him, to find out where he was going.

There was a shoeshine stand midway between Townsend's building and the corner, in an excellent position to watch the bus stop. Townsend was just in time to see the gray-clad figure digress from the crowd, step up on the rickety structure, and sit down in one of the two chairs it held. A striped canvas umbrella was poised over them to protect patrons from the sun. That sliced off the top of his head. An expanded newspaper, withdrawn from his pocket, screened the remainder. He became just an anonymous pair of legs raised to the foot rests of the shoeshine platform.

The attendant whipped out his flannel dusting cloth, crouched diligently to begin his task. Then he scratched his head and looked up at the outstretched newspaper over him a couple of times as if undecided what he was expected to do. The shoes must be newly burnished, probably didn't need a shine. But that wasn't why he was sitting there, Townsend knew.

Agate Eyes had only two fixed points to work from, so far, and he was making good use of them. One was that particular bus stop, which might be Townsend's usual embarkation point at the end of the day. The other was that around now might be Townsend's habitual time for reaching it. He could have been wrong on both counts. Townsend knew he was right.

His bus boarding point was lost to him for good; he'd have to skirt danger daily now, coming and going to work. He would have to use the bus line that fed the next avenue over, detour a block out of his way at each end.

He went back and left the building by another exit, and all the way over to the new bus stop his face was turned behind him more than before him. Every gray suit was an enemy until the pink oval above it had come into focus.

At home, drawing false courage from the security of his own walls close about him, he thought: Why don't I go up to him the next time I see him and demand to know what he wants with me once and for all? Why do I run away, when I don't know what I am running away from? It may be merely a mistake in identity. Why don't I at least stand my ground long enough to find out, the next time I catch sight of him?

But he knew that the next time he wouldn't. And the next time he saw the stranger again he didn't.

The pace of the chase was growing quicker. The radius of the contracting coils around him was growing tighter all the time.

Agate Eyes had found the building itself, the next time; entered it. And again Townsend avoided blundering into him by a hair's breadth. Incredible that such a miracle of split-second avoidance should repeat itself a second time—it violated all the laws of probability.

Townsend needed cigarettes, he found when he reached his morning's destination, stopped in at the cut-rate drugstore of his office building to buy them. While the cashier was counting out his change Townsend looked idly out through the window that revealed the lobby of the building.

The sight his eyes found was a segment of the same face he'd first seen three days before, passing by under a gray brim. Agate Eyes was talking to the elevator starter out there, close up against the drugstore show window.

The starter nodded, underlip pursed judicially. The panto-mime was as explicit to Townsend as though he'd been able to overhear the actual words. "Yeah, I have seen someone like that coming in and out the last few days. Must work here some place in the building." Townsend had only been back a week and the starter was new to him.

The agate eyes buried themselves deeper behind their lids with baleful calculation. The mouth under them asked some-thing, scarcely stirring its lips at all.

The starter shook his head in negation, waved a hand toward the unending trickle of humanity going by them, and shrugged helplessly. That said as plain as words, "So many people pass. You can't keep track of each and every one of them. You know how it is."

A voice suddenly sounded from across the counter, crumbled the rigidity that had held Townsend gripped until now. "Could I interest you in one of those? We got a special on them."

Townsend turned, walked quickly to the entrance, and flung out of the drugstore.

He gained the street and looked hauntedly back. No gray-eyed visage was peering after him from around the turn. He scuttled from sight. He'd made it. But he knew that was the end of his job.

He went on—fleeing before the unknown.

Easy enough to say to himself, "Face it! Find out what it is, once and for all! Make sure, at least, that there's something to be avoided, before you avoid it."

He couldn't. It was like jumping off into space from a great height. You may land safely and you may not; the one certain-ty is you can't get back on your perch again. Once he accosted this pursuer, he wouldn't be a free agent any longer. Whatever this man wanted of him, he'd never get away from him again once he put himself within his reach. There was a deadly tenacity about him; the way he'd chopped at that subway door with his gun butt showed that. This was no halfhearted pursuit, no casual badgering. This was a man hunt in every sense of the word.

As he neared his homeward stop, the thought of Virginia was an added anxiety. Should he tell her that he'd given up his job?

Why not wait? Why burden her with another worry? She'd had enough already. He could get another job and wouldn't have to go into his actual reasons for deliberately chucking this one. He could let her think that he'd found the new one more advantageous. Anyway, he didn't have to tell her right away. He'd stay out the length of his working hours, find a park somewhere, sit in it killing time.

He sat there on a bench, beside a winding path, with green, young spring grass dappled in the sun around him, with the peace of the setting doing its best to claim him and being buffeted back by the turmoil, the knotted tension, within. He sat there far forward on the edge of the bench, occasionally blowing through his hands as if to warm them, for the most part staring wanly down at nothing on the ground. The hours slowly circled past over his head.

But the problem had no answer, no relief. "He comes from That Time. He must, there's no other explanation, no other possibility. It's not a mistake in identity. He really knows me. But I don't know him. He's someone from the Three Forgotten Years." And that, he knew, was why he was really afraid. It was the aura of the unknown. He was no more of a coward than the next; he wasn't really afraid of the man, he would have braved him before now if that had been all there was to it. It wasn't physical cowardice, it was mental.

This man came out of the shadows, bringing them with him. This man was armed with an unknown weapon. There was a terrible remorselessness about his pursuit. Townsend could not bring himself to meet the challenge. He had just experienced a deep-reaching psychic shock, hadn't had time fully to get over it yet. He probably wouldn't get over it completely for years to come.

He was handicapped in being called on to meet fresh tests of spiritual courage at such a time. He needed peace; he needed safety. His lacerated psyche required time to knit itself together again. It was still jittery, sensitized, it needed a chance to convalesce undisturbed.

No one noticed Townsend sitting on the park bench all that day. A quiet figure, desperately trying to pierce the curtain that hid the past.

It grew later. The children began to hurry out of the park.

A random, homeward-bound nursemaid or two, wheeling her charges, followed after that, at intervals. The birds seemed to go too, or at least become voiceless. The sunlight itself started to withdraw from around him. The whole world was leaving the scene. The park became still, hushed, with a sort of macabre expectancy. The daily death of light was about to occur.

The things of the night began to slink into view. Blue shadows, like tentatively clutching fingers, began a slow creep toward Townsend out from under the trees. Deepening, advancing only furtively when they weren't watched closely, pretending to be arrested when they were. At first azure, scarcely visible in the still-strong light of day. Then dark blue, like ink rolling sluggishly amidst the grass blades and dyeing them from the roots up. At last, freed of the vigilance of the closing red eye of the sun, turning black, showing their true color.

One, the longest, boldest of them all, like an active agency trying to overtake him, to trap him fast there where he was, pointed itself straight across the path, advancing upon him by crafty, insidious degrees like a slithering octopus tentacle. He drew his foot hastily back out of its reach, as though it were something malign, with an intelligence of its own. He stared down at it with cold mistrust, watched it waver there frustrated, like a snake whose strike has fallen short.

Night. That meant night, that little brush stroke of black lying there athwart the ground. Night, the time of fear, the enemy.

He wanted to get out of here. He wanted to put walls around himself, light lights, shut doors. In palpitant awareness of the unseen he got up and moved along the winding path through the twilight. Only the slow dignity of his outer step was adult; inside he was a lost child moving through a scary array of goblin trees, with a lighted cigarette for protective talisman instead of crossed fingers.

4

HE DIDN'T like having to fool Virginia like this. He wanted to tell her. Several times he almost did, but then he checked himself each time. He hated to dump this on her, particularly because it was such a sketchy, formless danger. She'd had so much trouble already. Three years of it. Across the dinner table he could still see the traces of what she'd been through. Her eyes were sad. And she still didn't laugh as she had before he went away. You couldn't go through anything like that and not have it do something to you.

So he didn't tell her. Let her enjoy her peace while she had it.

Then, with a soundless flash that should have lighted up the silverware and dishes around him, came a sudden realization of renewed danger that had escaped him until now for some strange reason. His address here, his name, and all other pertinent information about him were on file down where he had worked, accessible to the most casual inquiry.

All through those vacant, staring hours in the park, that had never occurred to him. He had been an ostrich, burying its head while its tail plumes flaunted in the breeze.

It was the inevitable next step, too. Agate Eyes had found the building he worked in; that was today. By tomorrow he would find the exact floor. Then the right door on that floor. And once he had found that, he would painlessly extract the information of where Townsend lived. The pursuit would suddenly overleap the distance he had imposed on it, strike home here. And from here there was no easy retreat possible. Here there was Virginia. Here he was rooted fast.

He had just postponed the inevitable, gained a day or two at the most.

There might still be time. Time, that ally of all frightened things, ever since there first was fear. Maybe they could be persuaded to withhold his address, shield him.

He would have given anything to be able to get in touch with them then and there, get it over with; he would have felt that much safer before he went to bed and tried to sleep. This way he'd have an uneasy feeling that the wheels of pursuit were still grinding, somewhere unseen, all night long, while he lay in false security. He'd have to wait until the morning to reach them; there wasn't anyone down there after six. If he'd only thought of it in time, he'd had all afternoon long in which to do it, while he sat there idling in the park. He paced back and forth, as though trying to wear the night away, like a carpet is worn away by walking on it. But the evening's quarter hours went by no more quickly than if he'd been sitting patiently in a chair, and he saw that he was only making Virginia uneasy by his restlessness.

There was one hope: if he couldn't reach them during the night to protect himself, neither could his nemesis reach them during the night to extract any information out of them.

In the morning it was the first thing on his mind as his eyes opened—a held-back injunction from last consciousness, that flashed its way in like a ray of light when a door is first opened into a dark room. "Phone them fast, get to them before *he* does!"

He could hardly wait to gulp his coffee, grab his hat, and get out.

"But you're not late," Virginia tried to reassure him. "You're even five or ten minutes ahead of your usual time today."

He threw her a half-truth across his shoulder, "I know, but there's a call I've got to make the very first thing!"

He did it from the corner below. And, ironically, he was too early the first time. There was no answer.

He stayed by the instrument, palpitating, drumming his fingers. Then he swung the dial wheel around again and this time was answered by the familiar voice of the telephone girl.

There was a slight stiffness to her tone. Not of manner, but of posture, if such a thing can be visualized. As though she hadn't had time to take off her hat yet, and was leaning over the switchboard from the outside of the rail, rather than sitting before it at ease.

"Hello. That you, Beverly? This is Frank Townsend."

Her accents thawed to the proper intimate plane reserved for a fellow worker. "Oh, hello. What happened to you yesterday, Frank? You stayed out, I noticed. Weren't sick, I hope?"

"I'm not coming in any more, Bev," he said.

"Ah, I'm sorry to hear that, Frank," she lamented. "We'll all miss you. Boss know about it yet?"

"I'm mailing him a letter," he improvised.

"Well, lots of luck, Frank. And any time you're in the neighborhood, drop in and say hello. You know we'll always be glad to see you."

He said, "Look, Beverly, I want you to do something for me, will you?"

"Sure, Frank."

"Please, under no circumstances, give out my home address. I mean, just in case anyone should happen to inquire. I don't say anyone would—" He threw that in just to make it sound more plausible. "But just in case they should. You don't know my whereabouts, you haven't got any record of them, see?"

She wasn't curious enough to ask any questions. "I understand, Frank. You can rely on it. I'll tell Gert the same thing. We're the only two that know where to look for it in the files, anyway. Wait a minute, I'll make a note of it just to make sure." He could tell by a change in her voice that she was jotting down something as she spoke. "In future don't give out Townsend's address if you are asked for it."

Something like a cold spray buffeted him for a second. He didn't like that *in future*. "No one's asked *already*, have they?" he said, gripping the receiver.

She was blithely unaware of the catastrophe implicit in her answer. "Yeah, there *was* somebody in here yesterday afternoon, a little before closing time, but I'll make sure that from now on—"

The world—and the booth with it—went plunging into darkness, as though it were on a train passing through a tunnel.

She was saying, "Wait a minute, here's Gert now, I'll ask her. She was the one at the board at the time." A period of indistinct offside murmuring took place. Then her voice was centered forward again. "He came in at the very last moment, we were all getting ready to go home, and she couldn't lay her hands on it at the moment; you know five o'clock down here. So she gave it to him from memory; she doesn't know whether she got it right or not."

A shaft of silver pierced the leaden pall around him. Very

slender, very fragile, but struggling through. "Find out if she remembers now just what it was."

He could hear a clicking sound made by cogitating gum, in the background at the other end of the line, as the nonparticipating Gert brought her head down within range. His vis-à-vis resumed with a laugh: "She can't even remember that much now. You know Gert."

"Well, look it up and ask her if it's the same as the one she gave out."

"Wait'll I find it," she said. "It's around here some place." It took quite some finding, apparently, judging by the length of time he was kept waiting.

Then she came back again. "I've got it, Frank. Here it is here. Eight-twenty Rutherford Street, North. Is that right?"

His old address. The place Virginia had moved from during his absence. Through an oversight they'd never changed it when he came back to work again. He was safe; he was out of reach. Relief shot through him in an exquisite flood.

Meanwhile, a shriek of delighted contrition sounded in his ears as they compared notes at the other end. "That wasn't the one she gave him at all! She gave him Tom Ewing's by mistake, got it mixed with yours, sent him all the way out to—He'll have a fit when he gets out there! Who was he anyway?"

He said, with utter truthfulness, "I haven't any idea."

"Have we the right one down, Frank?" she went on, trying to be helpful. "Because they'll probably be sending you out a pay check for a half week on Sat'day and you want to make sure of getting it."

"Yes," he said firmly, "it's right." He'd stop by and pick it up at their old place. Mrs. Fromm would hold it and turn it over to him.

As he hung up the receiver he felt free, for the first time since he'd begun his flight from the menacing stranger.

An unfastened shoelace had saved him the first time. A pack of cigarettes had saved him the second time. A gum-chewing, addle-pated switchboard girl in a hurry to get home had saved him the third time.

He went back to the park again. A different bench, a different path, but the same peaceful, sun-gilded panorama around him. All he had to do was eye the distant skyline of serried building tops peering above the trees on three sides of him, and his sense of immunity immediately contracted by that much. It extended only as far as the green oasis of the park did, with danger still over there, somewhere, down in the chinks between those buildings.

He took off his hat, whipped it impatiently against the shanks of his legs as though there were gnats about him. "Danger! I keep saying danger! Danger of what? From what? What've I ever done to be endangered by?"

And, of course, there came the immediate answer again, inevitably, that was the crux of his whole reaction to the situation: "Three years is a long time. In three years you can do lots of things that bring danger in their train." And he knew that his subconscious, his innermost instinct, call it what you will, was more to be relied on in this case than all the logic his intelligence could bring to bear. This wasn't just surface fear; there *was* something to cringe from, to shrink away from.

His mind couldn't recognize it. Well, his mind had been dormant for three years. His subconscious was doing its level best to warn him. The only unfortunate part of it was his subconscious wasn't articulate, couldn't put it into thought phrases, couldn't tell him what it was.

Yes, he thought moodily, somewhere in that city, around the four sides of this park, there's a man whose only thought is me. Who is looking for me, up one street and down another, around this corner and beyond that, minute by minute, hour by hour. And sooner or later, since I am a more or less fixed object and he is in constant motion, he is going to find me.

Then why not go away to some other city? Why just change from one flat to another, and remain all the time in the same danger zone? Why not move out of it entirely?

They couldn't. All the reasons why people don't at their age entered into it. They didn't have very much money put aside, not enough to allow for a move like that.

And even if it could have been done successfully, it still wouldn't spell immunity, only postponement. *It* would always be here, waiting to pounce. *It* would always bar him from coming back here. Some day, eventually, *it* might even trace him from here, reach out after him to the new city.

The only thing to do was lick it on the spot. And how are you going to lick a thing when you don't know what it is? The circle of his meditations had completed itself; he was back where he had started.

Their old flat was still tenantless, he noticed, when he went there the following Saturday to pick up his pay check. The ghosts of their younger, happier selves, his and Virginia's, must still be lurking there in those empty rooms, they'd spent so much time in them.

He rang for Mrs. Fromm, stood waiting in the street entrance for her to come up from below. Someone else looked out at him inquiringly. Some other woman. "Did you ring?" she demanded.

"Yes, but I was looking for Mrs. Fromm. Isn't she here?"

"She doesn't work here any more."

For a minute he didn't recognize the fact for what it was worth. Then realization flooded in on him. This meant that, without his having to say a word, lift a finger, he was safe, immune, at this end. This newcomer, whoever she was, did not know their new address. She couldn't pass it on to anyone even if she wanted to.

His relief knew no bounds. It wasn't just a matter of hair's-breadth avoidance any more; he was cut off, beyond reach for good now. Well, always barring mishaps.

His homeward tread, retrieved pay check in pocket, had a lilt to it that had been missing since the shadowy nebulae had first descended. Fear was gone. Self-confidence was back. He even caught himself humming a little under his breath. It became a full-pitched whistle. He hadn't whistled since before the great blank. He didn't even know any of the new things to whistle. He had to whistle an old one. It didn't matter; it was good.

A man in a gray suit, with a gray hat aslant over his eyes, went by, almost grazed him, and he hadn't even remembered to be wary. He threw out his chest, widened his shoulders, resumed his whistling, and went on.

He passed a little bakeshop window and caught sight of a tray of cream puffs in it. Virginia had always had a weakness for them. He felt so good he stopped in and bought two of them, to take home to her. You have to be feeling good to buy things like cream puffs; they go with a carefree state of mind.

Maybe it was over now. Maybe he'd worked himself free from the pursuing shadows at last, put himself beyond their reach. Maybe he was safe, out in the sunlight from now on, to stay.

Always barring mishaps.

5

HE HAD to do a certain amount of juggling to conceal from Virginia that he had quit his job. The check wasn't payment for a full week, so he added to the envelope a proportionate amount out of his small reserve to make the correct total.

He couldn't, of course, do this a second time; he not only hadn't sufficient funds, but the next time the entire amount of his salary would have had to be substituted. But Monday he'd look for another job, and possibly by the next week end he'd have a bona-fide pay check to replace the former one.

Monday he did. Tuesday he did. Wednesday, Thursday, Friday. He looked in a way that applicants seldom do. He didn't go by the compensation offered, nor even by the suitability to his own previous experience. He went by geographical location; discarded those within the danger zone, those too close to the vicinity of his former place of work, fed by the same transportation facilities. He marked off and followed up only those addresses lying at a considerable distance and in an opposite direction, even when that entailed making trips into grimy, industrialized suburbs.

He found he was gyrating in a vicious circle. He needed references, and he was unwilling to refer to his last place, lest he reopen a means of tracing him to the new one.

He could have got references, but he daren't apply for them.

Several openings that he might have had slipped through his fingers for lack of credentials. Then the end of the week was upon him, and he was face to face with the necessity of telling Virginia the whole thing, bringing on the worry he'd been trying all along to spare her.

When he returned Saturday, his supposed payday, primed to confide the whole thing to her, he could tell by her face something was troubling her. "Frank, did your pay check come today? Was it in the letter box when you went out?" she began immediately, before he had a chance to say anything.

"No—"

"Then it's been lost in the mail, something's happened to it!" She rushed on. "It wasn't received over at our old address either. I was just around there to find out—"

Every muscle in his body tensed. "You were over there?"

"Only this morning I happened to pick up the envelope of last week's check—I came across it in the back of the bureau drawer—and just as I was about to throw it out, I noticed our old address typed on it big as life! You never told me you had to go over there and claim it. Well, I went over to make sure in case it went there a second time by mistake, it would be forwarded to us here—" She stopped when she noticed the look on his face.

"You gave that woman, the new janitress over there, our address *here?*"

"Why yes, I wrote the name and the address down for her on a piece of paper, so she'd be sure to remember it."

Always barring mishaps, he reflected, always barring mishaps.

6

HE COULDN'T sleep. Although he had dozed off for a short time immediately upon touching the pillow, it had been only a half sleep, troubled by a dream. A peculiarly grueling species of dream, though there were no distortions in it, no traumal goblin shapes. No complete persons in it at all. In fact, there had been nothing in it but a pair of feet and a patch of pavement just big enough to contain them.

They kept moving forward, toward him, toward the dreamer's eye, and the pavement they trod kept slipping past beneath them, like a treadmill going the other way. It was as though the dreamer were moving backwards, away from the feet, and the latter were following remorselessly.

The feet kept coming toward him, coming toward him, toes pointed straight at him.

There was more inchoate terror, more undiluted horror, in that simple undistorted pair of black-shod feet (never at a run, always at the same even, implacable, persistent walk) than in all the ogres, monsters, menaces, hooded forms of dream plasma put together. It was their quiet implacability.

They were as lifelike, as natural, as the moving pavement belt beneath them. They were heavy black brogues; they expressed beetling menace, somehow, by their very thickness and last alone. He could even see the worn breaks across their vamps. He could even catch the high lights glancing from their hubs as they rose and fell, rose and fell, with pistonlike regularity. He could even hear the slight, soft grate of straining leather they made each time—nothing so acute as a squeak—the cushioned thud of their incessant fall upon the pavement. The rhythm of the walk—*pat—pat, pat—pat—pat, pat—pat—pat, pat.* You hear the sound at night, when the streets are still, when someone's coming toward you in the distance.

Over them hung trouser legs, of some neutral color that didn't register—gray perhaps. They were naturalistically enlarged (not as to dimension, only as to detail), as through the magnifying glass that the whole dream view was. The cuffs at their bottom, their slight dip and rise over the shoes each time with the break of the unseen knees above, even their very woolliness of texture.

But it was the shoes that held the spotlight. They never faltered, never missed a step. It was as though they knew they needn't hurry, for nothing, no one, could escape them, feet so tireless, so persistent.

And slowly, unnoticeably, they began to gain on the retreating dreamer's eye, to come closer, closer, within the frame of vision that contained them. There was no escape. To turn aside and let them go by was impossible; the dream followed a fixed channel. They would only turn with the beholder, as if both operated on a single direction finder. The crevice between sole and pavement, opening and closing, was like a hungry maw now, grazing, threatening to trap and crush and trample the retreating, rigidly bound dreamer.

The frame shattered into unbearable light at the moment of

their finally breaking through it and overtaking him. He awoke from the dream.

He saw, in the slow reintegrating process of psychic cohesion, the knitting up of the intelligence where the ominous vision had come from. That pair of feet raised to the foot rests of the shoeshine stand. The image must have festered since then in his subconscious, finally worked its way free tonight. He had heard that this often happened; you dreamed about things that impressed you, not immediately after, but sometimes days, weeks later. And as for their dogging him so relentlessly, the portent was to be found in actuality rather than in the dream. Wasn't that what they *had* been doing?

Or was the portent that they were somewhere outside there on the surrounding streets right now, pacing through the night, coming toward him, drawing nearer footfall by footfall at this very minute, while he crouched in passive helplessness in his bed?

He touched a match to one of his unfailing nocturnal cigarettes, and Virginia's face, opposite in the other bed, stood out for a minute, a pale golden oval, then dimmed again. Her soft, regular-pitched breathing reached him through the dark. Thank God at least one of us can sleep, be at peace, he thought contritely. She had had her three years of wakefulness, while he— where had he slept, how had he slept, what dreams had troubled him then? Now it was his turn. She had earned her repose.

A jeeringly bright, and not particularly friendly, star was looking in at him through the window from the night sky outside.

He put his cigarette out and lay back and turned over. He couldn't go back to sleep. That dream had finished him. He turned the other way, then the other way, a hundred other ways, but he couldn't regain sleep.

Presently he felt like smoking again, wanted to move around.

He sat up and found his slippers. He didn't own a robe, so he put on his trousers instead, and felt his way toward the door, got it open without any noise, and closed it after him from the other side.

He put on a small light in the other room—simply so he wouldn't jar into anything and rouse Virginia—and started walking back and forth.

How long is this going to keep up, anyway? he asked himself. What am I going to do about it? I've got to do *something* about it sooner or later. I can't just—

He stopped by the window, looked out.

Suddenly the cigarette fell from his lips.

He jumped over to the wall, killed the light. Then he approached the window again, stealthily, edging up to it sidewise along the wall until he could look out—at what he thought he'd seen the first time.

There seemed to be a man standing there, directly opposite, facing these windows in a surveyor's line of directness. He was in the black silt of a shadow that filled a wall indentation like sand blown into a niche. It might have been just an optical illusion, giving the shadow's border the rounded likeness of a shoulder, then lower down a hipbone.

As he peered, trying to decide, a faint flow of motion had altered the silhouette. The rounded scallops of the shoulder, the hip, drew subtly inward, disappeared into the heart of the shadow mass, leaving a clean-cut knife line of dark that should have been there in the first place but hadn't been.

So that, by its very disappearance, what had caught his eye betrayed itself as being a reality. If it had been an illusion it would have remained in sight.

He had to get out of here. He had to get out of here fast. His last hiding place had been found at last. It was coming now. It was here. In fifteen minutes. In half an hour. It was upon him.

He tiptoed out and listened at the front door. There was a low voice murmuring somewhere beyond, as though some amorous swain were loitering out there in the hall taking a lingering leave-taking of his girl; only Townsend knew that it was no swain. That wasn't love whispering out there, that was violence and hate and very possibly death. *He* had others with him. They were all around the place, getting set, getting ready to rush it. Any minute now.

He swung around and looked toward the oblivious bedroom doorway, that contained all he loved in the world. "I've got to get her out of here," he thought distractedly. "I don't want her to get mixed up in it. I don't want it to happen in front of her— whatever it is."

He went into the darkened bedroom, leaned over her, found her ribboned shoulder. He pressed it gently, trying not to startle her too much. Then he shook it, more urgently, until she was fully awake.

"Virginia, can you hear me? Don't be frightened."

She sat up. The soft perfume of her hair was about him.

"You've got to get out of here. I want you to come with me right now. No, don't light up, they may be able to look in and see us through the back window."

She was on her feet now, a silken shadow beside him. "They? Who?"

"Just your coat. Here, I've taken it down for you. Just put your feet into shoes the way they are, there's no time—"

"Don't," she whimpered plaintively, "you're frightening me."

He sought her lips with his, to give her courage. "Do you love me?"

"How can you ask?" Her voice was a frightened whisper.

"Then will you trust me enough just to follow me blindly, without asking any questions? I don't know the answers myself. I only know what I'm doing is right. Ready? Come on."

He went back to the outside door again, she behind him, hair awry, face still half awakened within the towering circle of her red-fox collar.

Outside there was a sort of swelling quiet, like a balloon about to burst.

"I don't think we can make it this—" he started to murmur.

It went right through the two of them, as though a volley of blank cartridges had been fired off under their noses. It was something heavier, harder than fists. The door seemed to explode with impacts. It made the light bulbs jitter in the ceiling. It made a pottery thing on a table sing out with the vibration, carried to it along the floor and up the table legs. It was the earthquake of an attempted forcible entry. It was violence in its most ravening form. It was the night gone hydrophobic at their threshold. It was disaster. It was the end.

Too late now. She was going to be right in the middle of the whole thing, see things that those you love shouldn't be called upon to witness.

She huddled against him, terrified. She gave a wordless heave, that was like a bronchial seizure. "Who—? Who's doing that?"

"It's what I wanted to get you away from," he answered bitterly.

Violence flamed in his own mind, catching fire from the violence outside the door. He caught up a wooden chair by one leg, poised it overhead at blow angle. His face was an unbaked cruller of rage. "Bring this to you, will they? Let 'em come—!"

She caught at his arm, pulled it—and the chair—down again. "No Frank, no! Don't! For me, Frank!" And he saw, looking at her twisted, tearing face, that she was more frightened of his rage than she had been of theirs.

That did something to him, snapped him out of it, the sight of that fright of hers. To get her to safety should be his only concern, the hell with everything else.

He drew her back away from the door, arm protectively circled about her shoulder. Like a pair of blundering dancers in half embrace they went this way and that, looking for a way out that wasn't there. Taking three steps toward the hopelessly blocked front windows, then doubling back; three steps toward the bedroom window overlooking the rear court, then doubling back as the telltale grate of feet on the cement reached them, magnified by the sounding board of the enclosing walls.

"There must be some way, there's got to be—!" His grimace was that of weeping for her, but he wasn't weeping.

Three steps toward the kitchen—and then he went on, with only a momentary misstep, as it came to him at last. He threw open a high wooden oblong, like a cupboard cover, set in the wall, brought up the dumbwaiter. "Didn't you once say our building and the one next to it have a single basement between them? I may be able to get you up and out through the next house over."

She started wringing her hands at him in encouraging, prayerful pantomime. It was like talking close to a thundering waterfall.

He wrenched out the horizontal bisecting shelf; it was not fastened down, just wedged in over two supporting braces. "See if you can squeeze in. I'll hold the ropes so you don't shoot down too fast."

She backed in, huddled there, head pressed upward against the low top. He gave the control rope a half turn around one hand to keep her weight from plunging it down too fast. She teetered there, ridiculous in her fur collar.

"Frank, you're coming after me? You're not staying behind?"

"Right away, the minute you get off. Wait down there for me." He was wondering if there'd be time for a second trip. The wood of the door was beginning to splinter, the nails holding the hinges to squawk out, back at the other end of the hall. They must be using hatchets to it.

"Keep your head in, honey, so you don't hit it against the side of the shaft."

The pulleys started to whir, the rope to needle through his restraining hands as he paid it out. Her face went down out of sight, in a sort of hideous parody of entombment alive. The distance was mercifully short. It struck bottom, as gently as he was able to control it. He leaned over the opening, scared stiff she mightn't be able to get out at the lower end. No light showed, but a loose swaying reached him that told she had left it. He brought it up again fast, climbed awkwardly into it, posterior first, still hanging onto the control rope. He went down jerkily, plummetlike. The crash of their entry above, as the remnants of the door finally flattened before them, blended with the crash of his own striking bottom, obliterating it. He landed with a thud that jarred his teeth and smote his hipbones.

She was standing there holding the chute vent open for him. He came tumbling out on hands and knees to the basement floor level, two or three feet below the dumbwaiter bottom.

He struck matches to guide them through the surf of cellar darkness. His foot struck a discarded baby carriage, but its own wheels shifted it away without causing him to overturn across it.

Another time a small freshet of lumps of coal, piled in a corner, sidled down, punching his toes cruelly.

Overhead they could hear, with an eery sensation of unreality, the scurry of searching footsteps scattering from room to room, trampling through the flat. The sound came down blurredly through the flimsy horizontal partition. There must have been at least a half dozen of them, judging by the activity.

"They'll know," he murmured bitterly. "Your bed was still warm. They'll be down in a minute. Quick, darling, quick!"

"What is it, Frank, what is it?" she lamented, still unnerved.

They found the fireproof, nailhead-studded door that led up into the other building, guarded only by a lateral bolt. But on their side, fortunately, on their side. He got it open. Cemented steps faced them, making an angular turn. There was a night light somewhere up at their head. They trod warily up, he in the lead. The janitor's living quarters were located over in the other building, their own building, so one added hazard was eliminated. For economy's sake, the same boiler, the same furnace, the same basement, had been made to serve both houses. To some unknown contractor's parsimony, or limited allotment, they owed their chance of escape.

There was still another door bounding these stairs at their upper end. He opened it slightly, listened carefully for sounds of activity out in the hall beyond or on the upper house stairs. Silence. The hunt hadn't reached this building yet. They came out together like two wraiths, hands linked defensively—a hatless, collarless man and a frightened, bare-legged young woman in a fox-trimmed coat.

There was a low-powered wall light shining just within the street entrance. He broke hands, left her where she was, crept edgewise out toward it, inserted two fingers within the wire guard around it, and turned it until he had interrupted the current, plunged them into shielding darkness once more. The street loomed up more visible in contrast. He motioned her forward in the dark, and she must have seen the beckoning silhouette of his arm against the street. She came on.

"You go first. You have a better chance alone than with me. They don't know what you look like. Don't look back toward our place, and don't look around in here. Just walk toward the corner, minding your own business."

She took a preliminary step out through the outermost glass storm door, within the guiding circle of his arm. He craned his neck, but the street seemed empty of figures up toward their own entrance at the moment; he couldn't see a sign of activity, hostile or otherwise. He urged her gently forward, like someone teaching a child to walk unaided.

"Go on, honey. Go on, like I asked you to. Quick, in another minute it may be too late—"

A plaintive sob was her obedience. Then he was standing there alone, and she was striking out, her shoes making a quiet little ticking along the pavement. That slight, nervous hurry that a respectable woman always gives to her gait when obliged to journey unescorted on the street late at night—no more.

He lingered behind as long as he could, because she was far safer alone than if he should be detected following. Halfway to the corner she must be now. No hurrying figure went after her, to halt and question her. No discovering hail was raised.

But he couldn't stay here any longer. Any moment they were bound to discover the means of escape he had taken. It was incredible that they already hadn't found it; it was the only possible remaining way out of the apartment.

He drew in a breath of crucial decision, narrowly edged out

the door, and came through into the open. For a moment, before he turned, he could plainly see the pale oblongs, cast by his own lighted windows, lying flat on the sidewalk down that way. He faced up the other way, the way she had gone, and struck out. His spine was held unnaturally rigid with the fear of being overtaken, and he had to keep his neck muscles locked against the impulse to turn and look back. But the street was very dark, and in a few short paces he was already beyond range of recognition from a distance. The one street light between him and the corner was on the opposite side of the way. It left him a narrow causeway of gloom, beyond its outermost perimeter.

At the corner, just before rounding it, he did look back. He couldn't help it. That had been their home back there, that place so suddenly set upon and warred against. He could still, even at this distance, make out the pale cicatrices that were its lighted front windows. They were almost the only ones, even yet, that were lighted at this hour, though pairs of others were beginning to brighten here and there in their immediate vicinity, awakening to the noise.

He turned the corner, and the present became the past, the past became the present.

She had found a driverless cab and was huddled in it, waiting for him, a short distance around the corner. A lighted oblong near by marked an all-night lunchroom.

He went up to it from the far side, keeping it between him and the lunchroom. She wanted him to get in with her. She had the door open in readiness. He closed it again from the outside.

"No, Virginia, I'm not coming with you. Honey, you go back to your mother's, out of the city. You stay there until you hear from me, so I'll always know where to find you. Whatever happens to me, I'll know that you're safe. They won't connect you with that flat back there. You're Mrs. Virginia Townsend, whose husband disappeared three years ago; you haven't seen him since. Don't try to reach me or get in touch with me in any way, for your own sake. I'll see you again—some day. And whatever you hear, whatever it turns out this is about—give me a break in your own mind, like you always have before."

She seized his wrist with both hands. "No! Let me take my chances with you! Frank, I'm not afraid, I'm not a coward! What's a wife for? What's marriage for?"

He disengaged them gently but forcibly, gave them back to her. "Honey, when a guy falls into a sewer or cesspool, he doesn't reach up and pull those he loves best down in with him. Good-by now and do as I tell you if you love me."

Their lips met hungrily, almost furiously, through the open cab window. A tear from one of her lashes penciled down his cheek. He drew his head back by main force. "I'm going over that way. When you can't see me, start sounding the horn for the driver. Good-by, darling."

He shoved off into the anonymity of the night, half of him left behind now. In a few minutes a taxi horn peeped querulously once or twice behind him. A sound that you hear a hundred times a day and never think about twice. He'd never thought a taxi horn could hurt you in the chest like this one did.

He looked back, and a dwindling red mote of taillight was all that was left of his marriage.

He'd never known how fiercely he really loved her until now that he didn't have her any more. He looked back once more; even the taillight was gone. Now there was just himself and the night and the past.

He kept going, ticking off crossings like railway ties under his feet, until the factor of distance alone had secured for him a slight edge of immunity, if only for a while. Once he took out a cigarette, put it to his mouth without breaking stride. Then, at what he saw ahead, he flung it down without lighting it.

The cop came on slowly, inquisitive of all who passed.

He mustn't falter now, or shrink involuntarily, as they were about to cross one another, he and this stray patrolman. Here he came. Here he was.

Their eyes met. "Kind of chilly, isn't it?" he heard himself say unexpectedly.

The other's voice came back, already beyond him: "Yeah, it is, that's no joke."

The step receded. But that had been a tinder-box of suspicion that had just passed him, safely unignited. One stray spark, such as to quicken the step, to glance back, and—

As he strode on through the night, wearing it out, wearing it thin until the gray started to show through, his future course of action was slowly but finally and immutably taking form in his mind. Since the present held no safety, he must go back into the past, then, to find out why. Back into the past that had done this to him, to force it to retract or let it engulf him. Back into the past—if he could find it.

It was only a small chink so far, like the secret entrance to a bewitched garden in a child's fairy tale. It had only one street on it. Tillary Street. But if he could find his way back into it through there, he could push its boundaries back, widen them out all around him, until again they took in the whole world. His whole world.

Tillary Street. Tillary Street. A part of a coping had fallen and felled him, and the past had become the present, on Tillary Street.

Its mere geographical location, its physical aspect, was no good in itself, wouldn't help him. The way back into the past lay through the mind alone—the minds of others, like lighthouse beams through the fog, glancing across and lighting up his own mind.

Would he find that on Tillary Street? Had he just been passing through it at random, from somewhere else *to* somewhere else, that day? Had it been as meaningless to him even then as it was now? Or had he been a frequenter of it, had he lived on or around it, had it played a fixed part in the habits of his past? There was only one way to find out. By going back there and haunting it, like the ghost he was, until it gave him its answer.

The night was gone and it was lighter now, but it was also chillier. A wind as homeless, as forlornly seeking, as he was himself seemed to blow out across the steel-blue, mist-blurred, still-unawakened city. He turned the back of his collar up around his neck, and set his face toward Tillary Street—and yesterday.

There must be someone who would know him, along its reaches. He'd course along it every day, by the hour, up one side and down another, over and over, until at last some pair of eyes lit up in recognition, some voice said hello, some figure stopped to greet him.

The street plate at its mouth was like any other, one wing pointing one way, one the other. A flare of newborn sunlight, almost the very first to strike down below the huddled rooftops, caught on it and wavered hazily across the dark-blue enamel and white capitals, like a pinkish spotlight contending against the full daylight.

Back into the limbo from which he had come. A man looking for his other, his forgotten self.

TILLARY ST.

ONE WAY ONLY

BOOK II
The Curtain Lifts

7

THE ROOM was a ghost from some long-buried yesterday. "You going to be here long?" the weazened old rooming-house keeper asked.

If Townsend could have told him that, he would have known more than Townsend knew himself. Maybe only an hour or two, before they traced him. Maybe days, weeks. No, not weeks, unless he found some job around here to keep him going. He'd had exactly eight dollars and seventy-nine cents in the pockets of the suit he was wearing at the moment those blank-cartridge-like blows exploded against his door.

He said, "That depends on what you charge me."

The gnarled old man chafed his hands. "For a room like this it gives four dollars." He batted his eyes enticingly, to soften the blow.

Townsend moved back toward the doorway. "Four dollars is too much."

"All right, but look, you got the street. *Every* week you got clean sheets on the bed. Fresh running water, even." He went over to a corroded projection resembling a grappling hook, turned its encrusted handle with great difficulty, and a rumbling sound issued through it, followed by a thin coil of red-dish-brown fluid. "Must be using it downstairs." He tactfully wedged it shut again, but the trickle continued unabated for several moments afterwards.

"I'll give you two and a half for it," Townsend said, stepping out through the doorway.

"Take it, take it," the old man called after him.

Townsend came in again, peeled two bills off his slender ac-cumulation, added a coin to them, clapped the whole amount ungraciously into the old man's eagerly reaching hand. "Gimme a key."

His new landlord grumbled under his breath at such an un-heard-of luxury. "A key he wants. What next?" He tried out sev-eral from his pocket, finally found one that fit, left it in the door.

Townsend, left alone, went over to the bleary window and stood looking down, sunlight escaping through the gap at the side of the shade, making a bright chevron on his sleeve. So that was the new world down there. He'd already walked once to the end of the world and back, before coming up here. The world was not very long; four blocks all told. Tillary Street only ex-tended from Monmouth to Degrasse. It stopped dead at both ends.

Their heads down there were like ants, swarming over dun-colored sand, going every which way at once, forming into black accumulations around each of the pushcarts that rimmed both curbs in a nearly unbroken line. The street had very little vehicular traffic, both because of this fact and because of the shortness of its length. It didn't lead anywhere in particular. An occasional agonized motor conveyance threaded its way through at snail's pace, horn sounding every moment of the way.

He'd rest awhile first and then go out again. He hadn't had

any sleep the whole of the night before. It already seemed so long ago and far away. He loosened his tie, took off his coat, hung it across the back of the chair.

He lay down on the bed, intending just to relax for a few minutes. Before he knew it the street cries had become somnolent, filtered in through the window, pleasantly lulling, not harsh and discordant any more. Then they all blended into one purr, and he slept his first sleep of the new life.

When he awoke it was already midafternoon. He tried the stubbornly resistant spigot handle over in the corner, and the whole section of pipe quivered and sang out. He found that as far as quantity went, the condition his landlord had referred to as "being used downstairs" was of a permanent nature. But after several minutes of steady leakage the trickle had at least rid itself of rust particles and become colorless enough to use.

He locked his door after him, more as a reflex from former habit than anything else, and outside it found himself assailed by a delayed odor of cookery that must have taken several hours to creep up from the ground floor where it had originated at noon. It reminded him he was hungry. Even ghosts have to eat.

One thing he noticed, on his way down the stairs, and it was a happy augury. That horrible sense of moral guilt he had felt last night had vanished. If this was the "feel" of the past—and of course it couldn't altogether be, for he wasn't actually immersed in the past yet—then it argued that he had either been guiltless or had owned an unusually impervious conscience. There was a continuing sense of danger, but it was the exhilarating not the depressing kind. It had a lacing of adventure in it, too. Perhaps it was because Virginia was out of the picture, all sense of responsibility had been lifted from him, and he had only his own fate to work out.

He walked a block down from his rooming house, which was near the Degrasse Street terminus of the street, and chose a food stall that seemed the likeliest candidate for whatever neighborhood trade there was. He decided this point simply on the strength of the number of refuse receptacles he glimpsed within the crevice leading back to its kitchen door. If they had that much garbage to dispose of after the day had ended, they must have a fair-sized turnover. At the moment, of course, there was no one in it. The Tillary Street section didn't have enough per-capita wealth to be able to indulge in between-meal snacks.

He kept eying the back of the counterman's head, after he'd perched himself on one of the tall pivot stools, and wondering: "Did I ever eat in here before? Would he remember me if he looked more closely than he did just now?"

He took off his hat, in order to clear his upper face of shadow. Then he thrust his face an inch or two forward above the counter, so that it couldn't fail to impinge on the employee's line of vision when he turned back from the glistening nickel boiler. The counterman's glance swept over him, but nothing happened. The man's mind was on the order he was filling. In any case, Townsend realized, he would have had to be an habitual customer in the past for outright recognition now to take place. He might have come in here before, but he might have come in here only once or twice, and people like this had faces before them day after day.

He asked the counterman finally, "How long you been working in this place?"

"Couple of weeks now, chief," the latter said.

Townsend thought grimly there goes the first chance.

He mapped out the preliminaries of his campaign while he sat there stirring grayish sweetening into the already thick sediment at the bottom of his cup. At each and every meal, he would patronize a different eating establishment along here. It wouldn't take long to run out of them, for there were not more than four or five along Tillary Street. He must try for recognition on the part of the employees or some of the customers. That would be one line of attack.

A second would be to enter, one by one, every store and shop along the entire four-block length of the street, on some excuse or other, try for recognition on the part of the storekeepers. Ask to be shown things they weren't likely to have in stock, or if they did, linger haggling, then finally walk out dissatisfied, after having remained long enough to determine whether he had ever been in there before.

Both of these were secondary; he was still pinning his main hope, of fairly sharp personal acquaintanceship, to the random pavements outside. For even recognition by sight, in an eating place or in a shop, didn't necessarily imply that the person doing the recognizing would know anything important concerning him. Simply that he had been in there once or twice before. Not his name, nor where he lived, nor who his friends were.

He couldn't, of course, afford to neglect any entering wedge, no matter how slight or ineffective it might seem. Even that sort of blanket recognition would be better than nothing at all; it would be a beginning, a point of contact. He wouldn't be suspended, as he was now, in a complete vacuum.

He came into the street, and when he replaced his hat, left it well back on his head. Then he continued down toward the Monmouth end of the street, still three blocks away. He moved slowly, with such sluggish lethargy of pace that there was no one in motion around him, whether man, woman, or child, who wasn't going faster than himself. Anyone glancing at him, in doubt the first time, would have ample time to look twice, verify his identity in case they were uncertain.

In any case, his rate of progress wasn't as great a concession as it would have been in another part of town. Really rapid progress along swarming Tillary Street would have required exhausting dexterity. The customers or window shoppers doubled up before the pushcarts clogged one side of the already inadequate sidewalk. The gossiping groups, static doorway loungers, and potential purchasers coming out of shop entrances to view bits of merchandise by benefit of daylight blocked the other. A tortuous lane of clearance was left between, but even here no precise keep-to-the-right rule was maintained; everyone seemed to go in whichever direction had happened to occur to him at the moment. The only factor that made the situation tolerable was that tempers down here seemed to be a good deal more even than on the more streamlined streets uptown. The poke of an elbow, an overstepped toe or trodden-on heel, went unnoticed, drew no angry, challenging glare. They also, incidentally, went unapologized, perhaps for that very reason. It was the apology itself, no doubt, that would have drawn the resentful, incomprehending stare.

Although he didn't time himself, it must have taken him a full thirty minutes to traverse those three remaining blocks. At the end of that time he was back at the Monmouth Street end once more. He crossed over to the opposite sidewalk and started slowly to work his way back.

The sun was starting to crimson and go down, and vacancies began to appear along the curb, as the more successful of the pushcarts, emptied down to a point beyond which nothing further could be hoped for, furled tents and broke ranks. Women appeared at windows high aloft and screeched down into the still-swarming depths to their children to come up. Their calls, like mystic wave lengths, all seemed to reach the right ears and elicit, if not obedience, at least squalling recalcitrance and objection.

The street had definitely thinned out by the time he found himself back at Degrasse again, although it was still overpeopled, and was the sort of a slum street that probably never was actually lifeless at any time of the day or night. He re-crossed to his original, to what by payment of two and a half dollars he was entitled to call "his own," side of the street, and stopped to rest awhile and try his luck from a motionless position.

His feet felt worn and dusty from the slow, unnatural shuffle he had held them to, a gait that is always more trying than an energetic walk. He had drawn one or two cursorily questioning looks during his long maiden voyage down the street and back, but he had to admit there had been nothing personal, nothing immediate, in them; they had probably been elicited by the "foreignness" of his attire (in a general, not specific sense) and bearing. He was still, even after the wear and tear of his night flight through the streets, slightly too formal for this neighborhood. It was a hard thing to put his finger on; it had nothing to do with cut or fabric. He tried to correct it, insofar as he was able, as he stood there, by the composite impression he gained from scanning a cross section of the locality's adult male population as it drifted back and forth before him. The discrepancies, which he remedied then and there, were minor ones in detail, important only in the general effect they conveyed. He unbuttoned his vest and allowed his shirt to peer through the gap of his open coat, as though he wore no vest. For the rest, it was mostly a matter of shifting his tie to hang a little less dead center and allowing his shirt to fit a little less trimly into his trousers. His suit still showed too apparent a crease, but that was a matter the passage of days would automatically remedy.

Presently it had grown dark, and Tillary Street came on with its lights. Though the gleam behind many of the upper windows was the greenish pallor of gaslight; there was no lack of oversized naked-glass display bulbs in the shop and stall fronts at sidewalk level, of almost bombshell-like brilliance, sizzling and spitting with their own power. One or two of the surviving pushcarts, remaining to do business to the bitter end, even lighted gasoline flares. The street took on a sort of holiday guise. If you didn't look too closely it even seemed gay, scintillant.

He stayed on awhile, hoping he'd have better luck after dark than during the daylight hours. Like a mendicant begging alms he stood there begging a donation of memories, but the obliviousness of those about him only increased rather than lessened.

Finally he turned and moved off, went upstairs to his room. He raised the shade, and the lights from below, even at this height, were sufficient to cast a luminous repetition of the window square past him at the other side of the room, bent in two, half flat upon the ceiling and half upright on the wall. He sat there on the edge of his bed, a dejected, shadowy figure. And once, at some break in inner fortitude—like a split in a film running through a projection machine, quickly spliced together again and resuming its evenness in a moment—his head suddenly dropped into the coil of his arms.

Then he raised it again, and that didn't happen any more.

It isn't easy to start life over at thirty-two. Particularly when it's a life doomed even before you take it over, and the time limit is subject to call without notice.

His indirect lighting blanked out without any warning when

a chronic "last-day" rummage sale directly opposite his rooming house dimmed for the night. He could have lit the gas jet in the room, but there was nothing to be seen, nothing to use it for.

He took off his shoes and lay back, and pulled something that felt like the rough side of a piece of sacking up over his underwear-protected body. Tillary Street dimmed like the unreal lantern slide it was, into the blankness of sleep.

His first day in the past hadn't paid off. He was still lost between dimensions.

8

A HEARTBREAKING near-hit occurred the following afternoon. He was on about the third lap of his thoroughfare-long pere- grination for that day, and the street had reached a three-o'clock climax of hurly-burly. There couldn't have been anyone left with- indoors, judging by the numbers choking its sidewalks and gut- ters. While he was breasting this tide like a tired swimmer, he suddenly felt himself clapped from behind on the shoulder by someone in transit, and a voice called out in gruff heartiness, "Whaddye say there?"

He had been looking over to the other side at that moment, and even in the brief flash of time it took him to swerve his head around, the unknown greeter had already blended indis- solubly into the crowd. He couldn't tell which one of those im- mediately ahead of him it had been. None were turning to look back, to see if the salutation were acknowledged. The direction of the roughly friendly hand and the trailing direction of the brief snatch of voice that had accompanied it told him that the person had been going the same way he was, but at a good deal faster gait; therefore he was before and not behind him by now. That was all. He hadn't thought quickly enough to call out an automatic answer, which would have been the only sure way of fixing the greeter's attention on him an extra moment or two. He had been taken too much by surprise.

Here was the chance contact, the thing he had been hoping and praying for, and which might never recur, slipping through his fingers. He ran ahead, desperately accosting those in the lead of him one by one, pulling them around short by their sleeves and coat edges, demanding breathlessly: "Say, was that you just now? Did you just wallop me on the shoulder?"

All he got was dull, uncomprehending shakes of the head. But somebody had done it, somebody must have! It had been a good, solid impact. He was about ready to fly with crazed helplessness, when suddenly the fourth man he tackled answered with somewhat sheepish reluctance: "'Scuse me, I mistook you for somebody else. You fooled me from the back for a minute." He pried his sleeve away from Townsend's convulsive grip and went on.

Townsend stopped dead for a minute while the sluggish tide of humanity flowed on around both sides of him; the sudden letdown was so cruelly deflating.

It had been on a Monday, a Monday-morning daybreak, that he had first reached Tillary Street. Tuesday passed and Wednesday; Thursday, Friday, and Saturday. Those first few he was sure of. After that they began to telescope themselves a little, lose their sharpness of identity. It was harder to keep track of the days down here. Having no job might have had something to do with it, or the blurring monotony of the routine he had set for himself. There came the day when his landlord accosted him at the foot of the stairs on his way out, and he knew he had been there a full week and it was Monday again.

He had been eating very sparingly and irregularly, but he discovered when he tried to pay for the coming week that he had only two-odd dollars left.

He handed over two, said, "I'll have the other fifty for you by tonight or tomorrow," wondering to himself at the same time how he'd manage to.

But he did have it by that very night, when he returned toward midnight; handed it over with finger tips puckery and red from long immersion, after an agonizing afternoon- and evening-long session washing the dishes in that place he'd eaten in the day of his first arrival. They had had a temporary need for someone, luckily. There was enough left to tide him over the next day or two, but he knew that, however else he managed, he'd never wash a dish again as long as he lived. He could still feel the greasy scum of reeking water, lapping up his arms to the elbows, for days afterwards.

He'd already finished his casing of the shops several days before this. And although he'd left a bad impression as a time waster, maybe even as a potential shoplifter, on many of the proprietors, and got dirty looks from then on whenever he strolled past their premises, he had nowhere gained the impression that any of them had seen him before.

His clocklike pacing of the street, day after day, up one side, down the other; then down the one, up the other, was undoubtedly making him familiar by sight to dozens of the denizens of Tillary Street, but it was all current familiarity, none from before, and to keep from getting tangled up and mistaking the one for the other, he held himself strictly aloof from overtures of new vintage, rebuffed them where they seemed about to be tentatively put forth for the first time.

Eventually, of course, a law of diminishing returns was going to set in against him. If he stayed on around here long enough for new familiarity to become seasoned, a time would come when he would no longer be able to differentiate recognition having its inception in the immediate past from that of the more distant past that he was trying to re-enter. But that point hadn't been quite reached yet.

He was haunted now at times, alone in his barren room at nights, with the ghost window square cast by the street lights wavering on the wall before his eyes, by a looming sense of failure, of the futility of the whole thing he was attempting.

Perhaps it was based on a faulty premise in the first place. He might have just been traversing Tillary Street at random, that day that the curtain had suddenly been drawn upon the past; might have happened upon it in the course of a haphazard, meaningless digression. He might be mistaking an erratic diversion for his regular orbit. How was he ever to find out, in that case, where he had been going or where he had come from? He might be just a block or two from a sector that would have paid him real dividends if he had begun to investigate it. Or he might be the whole span of the city away.

Or even suppose his premise was the correct one, and Tillary Street had played a fixed part in one phase of his past life? Even so he was relying on the laws of chance, of coincidence, wasn't he? And they might just not work out in his favor. For instance, suppose the one or two people around here who could have reoriented him had themselves drifted away by now? If they weren't around here any more, then the street was no earthly good to him just as a street. Or those who had had reason to seek him out down here, if there were any such, might have already done so—during the interim of his absence. Not finding him, they might take it for granted he was gone for good and would never come back to Tillary Street. He might stay here a thousand years without ever getting a glimpse into that unknown past.

One night, hopeless with continued lack of success, he charted a rough map of the immediate vicinity and tried to determine by a rough system of surveying just which near-by points of departure and destination might use Tillary Street as a short cut, or timesaver, or line of least resistance. But it wouldn't work out. Too many outside factors, that were still beyond his knowledge, entered into it. He would have had to know what his own former habits were, the nature of the errand he had been on at the time, and so on. He didn't know any of those things. In itself, as a mere geographical convenience, the use of the street as a short cut seemed to be ruled out. You could go down the parallel streets on each side of it just as quickly and a very great deal farther. It led from nowhere to nowhere. It began where it did for no reason and ended where it did just as irrationally, after four blocks of existence. It wasn't even a diagonal or transverse linking two nonparallel points; it adhered to the same foursquare pattern as all the other intersections about it.

He crumpled up the sheet of paper and threw it away, after long, laborious hours of struggle. The past wasn't easy to regain. There were no road maps showing you which way it lay. And meanwhile time was running out.

Although his lodging was taken care of for a while yet, the residue of the dishwashing money petered out within two days. He struggled on for another twenty-four hours after that without a penny, living on gratuitous cups of coffee slipped across the counter to him, when the boss wasn't looking, by employees of the various places where he had been a paying customer until now. They couldn't be expected to repeat that more than once, however. Tillary Street lived on a shoestring, and the five cents would have been taken out of their own wages if they had been detected. The fortuitous circumstance of a restaurant being without a dishwasher, or a shop being without a sidewalk barker at the precise moment when he needed a job, didn't recur a second time and wasn't likely to. That had been just a freak of timing. He wasn't looking for permanent employment—he had his full-time job cut out for him—so he didn't go out of the neighborhood. And in it, there was nothing to be found. But still he had to eat. The first day, already, of this forced abstention he was starting to feel hollow in the pit of the stomach and weary at the back of the legs as he prowled his useless, elusive beat.

He'd had all along, and still had, on him that flashy-looking cigarette case that had turned up in his pocket on this very street after the accident that day. He had kept it on his person all the weeks he'd been back living with Virginia, instead of hiding it away somewhere in the flat. Possibly to spare her the worry the sight of its strangeness might have caused her if she'd found it. It had accompanied him automatically the night of his flight, and it was the only thing on his person now that had even a potential intrinsic value. So he decided he'd try to raise something on it. He had no idea of its probable value, but it might help to tide him over another week or two, and meantime, any day—any day—

There was, strangely enough, no pawnshop located anywhere along Tillary Street itself, but he found one about a block and a half down Monmouth Street, to the right. He pushed his way into its camphor-reeking interior, empty at the moment, took out the case, blew on it, and polished it against his coat sleeve.

The pawnbroker, attracted by the sounds of entry, came out of a storage room at the back, gave him the sharply appraising look of his kind as he advanced along the inside of the counter

to the point where Townsend stood. "Well?" he said noncom-
mittally.

Townsend passed him the case, winged open, through the
small orifice in the wire mesh that separated them.

The broker made no effort to test it, weigh it, examine it closely
in any way. Townsend should have noticed that, but for some reason failed to. The technique of hocking was new to him.

Suddenly the broker had spoken, casually in intonation but
with explosive implications. "This again, hm?" he said weariedly.

Townsend wasn't expecting it. He was caught off guard, inattentively off guard. It was like flashlight powder going off. It's
over with before you even have time to jolt. He blinked as the
meaning hit him, then he paled a little, then he gripped the
edge of the counter a little tighter. This *again*. *Again*. He had
that sudden, strange, glimmering sensation that comes when
you've been in a pitch-dark room and a door begins to waver
slightly open, admitting the first peering light backing it.

He must have been in here with this same case before.

His voice shook a little, much as he tried to steady it. He tried
to make himself sound plausibly forgetful, no more. "Oh, uh,
was this the—the same place I brought it to before? All hock-
shops look alike to me." He hoped this didn't sound as lame to
his vis-à-vis as it did to himself.

The broker sniffed disdainfully. "I ought to know this case
by heart already. Three times you been in here with it now, haven't you?" Meanwhile he was holding it extended as if in rejec-
tion. Then, with an inconsistent time lag, his offer followed. "All
right, four dollars."

Townsend saw an opening, and clutched at it desperately.
"That wasn't what you let me have on it before."

The broker immediately took professional umbrage. "So

what're you going to do, argue? Four dollars is what it's worth. Why should I give you any more this time than the time before? It ain't any more valuable to me now than it was then, is it?"

Townsend's voice was tense. "Do you keep the—the ticket stubs, or whatever you call 'em, after the article's once been redeemed? I mean the part that the customer signs his name and address on, and that you hold until the loan is repaid?"

"Sure. You want me to look it up? What do I have to look it up for? I know this case by its pattern. I tested it for you before. Look at that." He showed him a little mark made by the drop of reagent acid. Townsend had thought it was a worn spot. "So you were raising a big holler, remember? Fourteen carat you tried to tell me it was. Silver, gilt. Four dollars."

Townsend was pleading almost abjectly by now. "Well, just to convince me, just to make sure. Go ahead, see if you can dig it up. I just want to see with my own eyes."

"You telling me I don't know my own business? I ought to know how much a piece of security is worth to me." The pawnbroker was maddeningly interested in the question of the amount involved. "When were you in here with it last?"

He'd come back to Virginia on the tenth of May. He took a chance, faltered: "In April, this year. Look it up in your ledger, you must have it down."

The broker went into the back again, snapped on a light. There was a long wait. For Townsend an agonizing one. He was leaning against the counter, letting its edge cut into him across the middle, as though the physical hurt dulled the other torment.

"April eighteenth," the broker said suddenly, from inside. "Silver-gilt cigarette case. Black enamel, silver stripes. Ticket Number mumble-mumble—*four dollars*. Was I right?"

"Bring the canceled ticket out, I want to see the canceled ticket," Townsend called. There was a desperate urgency in his voice.

The broker came back with an oblong bisque pasteboard and looked at him curiously. "Here. Maybe you'll tell me now I'm wrong. Is this you or isn't it?"

Townsend cocked his head to match the angle at which the pawnbroker was holding the stub, searching for the penned fill-in on the printed form. The handwriting wasn't recognizable as his, but that was to be expected. If memory wasn't transferable, nothing was.

The name was George Williams, and he knew at sight that it was spurious. Something about it, it was too glib, too pat. Not that there weren't people called George Williams, but *he* hadn't been. His hatband had been initialed D N. The address was down as 705 Monmouth Street. Was that also fictitious, to match the name? There was a chance it hadn't been.

"Well, what about it? You want to turn it in or not?" the pawnbroker called after him sharply, as he made for the door.

"Be back later," he said, and gave the half doors a fling that must have kept them banging in and out for minutes as accompaniment to his footsteps racing away.

He hustled up Monmouth Street toward the seven-hundred sector. 700. Pretty soon now. One of those just ahead.

He came to a spasmodic halt, went on a few faltering steps farther, as if by reflex momentum, then stopped for good. There wasn't any 705. The one before it was 703. The one after it was 707. It was a public bathhouse.

The door had slammed shut. The room was dark again.

9

THREE DOLLARS and seventy cents later, toward five in the afternoon, he was coursing his beat again when Tillary Street suddenly started to drain of people around him. He didn't count time by days and hours any more, but by the pennies that controlled his purpose. He was within thirty cents of destitution again, and nothing further left to pawn. One more day's subsistence, even by his own frugal standards.

He was halfway down his beat, on the Watt-to-Jordan Street strip, when the usual afternoon crush on the sidewalk started to siphon off around the corner ahead and into Watt Street. There had been the jangle of fire apparatus a moment or two earlier, coming from up that way, and there were intermittent wailing additions to it from time to time after the exodus had got well under way. Kids started it first, darting off with whoops from under people's legs. Then their elders all started to converge after them, at gaits varying from lopes to waddles. It caught on like a panic, though it was for this neighborhood a joyous event, a means of self-expression, almost a social occasion. Suddenly the whole population was streaming en masse toward that one point of the compass. Only the pushcarts and their duty-bound guardians remained, the former looking strangely naked on the asphalt solitude.

Townsend wasn't going to allow himself to deviate at first. What was a fire to him, or any other outside interruption that had no direct bearing on his trancelike purpose? But then, because the very emptiness of the street before him robbed his further progress of any usefulness, at least for the time being, he turned and followed slowly in the wake of the rear guard. But at a detached, unhurrying stroll.

There was a haze of bluish-gray smoke visible in the middle distance, about two blocks up Watt Street. You couldn't get any nearer than a block away from the actual site. The overflow, from Tillary and all the other streets around, evidently held back by ropes near the point itself, had dammed up and jelled into a solid mass of humanity stretched across the street from side to side, with little shifting fringes.

He came up behind this, but stopped a few feet off, still in the clear, remained there on the outskirts. The only concession he made to curiosity was to crane his neck to try and see over the heads of those in front of him.

He had come to a halt before a house front. There was nothing remarkable in that. There would have been a given house flanking him at any point along the street. Every one of the windows, in that and every other house, was brimming with hopeful onlookers. Only in this one there was a kid mangling an orange in one of the top-floor line of windows. Someone happened to jostle the kid, and something viscous jarred Townsend's shoulder, glanced off, landed with a soggy spat on the ground before his feet.

He shied skittishly back, turned to look up and identify the culprit. His face looked steadfastly upward with resentful intensity for a long minute. A face upturned like that attracts the eye from above, even the eye fixed elsewhere, out into the distance.

A voice suddenly keened out from somewhere along the building front, thin against all that street hubbub and commotion but flutily audible just the same, *"Dan!"*

And the past had opened to admit him at last.

10

AT FIRST, as he quickly corrected his angle of vision, brought it down window tier by window tier, all he found was a sudden blank spot, where a face had been amidst all the other faces. The center window, on the second tier, was where the hole was. But the face itself had gone before he could locate it; it was only its absence that registered. The surrounding ones quickly pressed in to fill the gap and then even that was gone.

He knew the cry had been meant for him, but that was by sheer instinct alone. It had been "thrown" directly at him, not to the right and not to the left; the intensity of vibration caught by his eardrum somehow told him that. Whoever had emitted it was probably on the stairs inside the house, on her way down to him, at that very moment.

He stayed there where he was, rooted there, rigid there. Afraid to think that this again might be a blind alley. A crushing sense of irony had overcome him. Whether false or true, this was undeniably recognition, and recognition had lurked *one block off* Tillary Street all this time, while he paced back and forth there endlessly, in sight of this very house each time he spanned the open width of Watt Street, just up there at the next corner.

Seconds had never seemed to last so long before. He was palpitating from head to foot, inside, just below the skin. Who was this going to be? What was it going to be? And if he were accosted, as he almost certainly was about to be, would it be by friend or enemy?

What was he to say? How was he to find out what he might be expected to say? A warning inner voice kept adjuring him: Keep cool now. Don't lose your head, whatever you do. Keep your self-control, because every gesture, every syllable, will count for something; make sure you don't miss anything. Say very little yourself. Say as little as possible. Rather too little than too much. Rather nothing than the wrong thing. *Feel* your way, like a blindfolded man walking a tightrope.

Maybe a minute had gone by. Maybe ninety seconds at the most. It seemed like hours ago that that despairing cry had winged down to him. He had put his hand to the worn iron doorstep rail that led outward to him, and it vibrated ceaselessly even on that; he couldn't hold it still.

Suddenly the house entrance discharged a careening figure like a shot out of a sling, and she was up to him eye to eye before he could even take her in in any kind of decent perspective. His visualization of her had to spread outward in concentric, radiating circles from those eyes, staring into his at such close range.

Brown eyes.

Bright brown eyes.

Tearfully bright brown eyes.

Overflowingly tearful bright brown eyes.

Suddenly a handkerchief had come up to shut them off from him for a moment, and he was able to steal a full-length snapshot of her. Not much more.

She was young. She was slim, a little better than medium height for a girl. The clean, white-looking side part of her hair came up to the lobe of his ear. Her hair was brown, without any blonde in it, without any red in it, with a bronze shimmer to it. She wore it down the nape of her neck in a waterfall. She was bareheaded, for she had come running down from upstairs just as she was. She wasn't pretty but she was anything but plain. Her face was vibrant with animation and warmth, to take the place of conventional beauty.

She was—But that was it, who?

The handkerchief had come down again, and inventory was over. He had to be satisfied with what he'd got, there was no chance for any more right then.

Her first words were, "Danny! I never thought I'd see you again!" She was as close to him as she could possibly be, so this was no mistake. He was Danny, Danny to stay, that was his name in the living past, the *present* past. He thought irrationally that he'd always hated that name.

"Oh you fool! You crazy fool! What are you doing out on the open street like this! Have you lost your mind?"

He spoke for the first time. He began life all over again with her—whoever she was. "Watching the fire," he said quietly. Not too much, not too little.

She looked up one way, she looked down the other. She looked around on the outside of them, in a sweeping half circle. She was plainly worried—for him. "What's the matter with you? Don't you know crowds are the worst place for you? You never can tell when one of *them's* likely to be in them, looking around for just such people as you!"

One of them. Just such people as you. She must know about it. Something about it, anyway. How much did she know about it? The whole thing? Part of it? How? Directly? Indirectly?

Something neutral. Find something neutral to say, because he couldn't just stand there dumb, that would be dangerous too. He let his eyes flick upward toward the window from which her voice had come, then brought them down to her again. "You've sure got good eyesight."

"I ought to know you by now, from any distance." She said it in a scathing, depreciating sort of way. The lantern of her face glowed dark for a minute, as if with remembered hurt.

Townsend was afraid to risk a question. "Yes, I guess you ought to," he said evenly.

"Well, what are you going to do, stand out here in full sight, in the broad daylight, until someone comes along and picks you up?" In her concern, she began to pull him by the sleeve, inward toward the doorway. Her voice sharpened with resentful anxiety. "What are you trying to do, throw yourself away? Come in! Come in the hallway, at least!"

He followed her into the narrow passage leading back to the stairs, and the glare of the afternoon toned down to twilight. They stopped halfway back along it, both against the same wall, faces toward one another. His back was to the street.

He took a chance, slithered a foot out along the tightrope to see if he couldn't make a little headway. "You—you seem kind of worried about me."

Her hand switched up and slapped him across the mouth. That question, evidently, was inflaming to the hurt and grievance he thought he'd detected before. Even that didn't seem to be enough of an outlet. She suddenly clenched both hands and pummeled him on the chest. She couldn't hit very hard. Or maybe her resentment wasn't unmixed enough to allow her to. "You devil! Oh you lowdown devil! Why do I love you like I do?"

Suddenly, in place of one of the battering fists, her head had come forlornly to rest against him. Just for a brief moment. Then she raised it again. "Oh, Danny, why'd I ever meet you? Why'd I ever have to know you at all?"

What is this I've run into? Townsend wondered, appalled. What have I been doing to this girl?

"You're no good," she said. "You never will be any good—" And then, without a change of inflection, at the sound of a descending step on the stairs, "Quick! Come back here underneath the stairs, where everyone coming in and going out doesn't bump into you!"

She came with him and they cowered there, in still closer, dimmer confinement. They waited in silence until the tread had gone out into the open. She looked out to make sure, then turned back to him again, in heightened solicitude. "Where are you now, Danny?"

There seemed to be a good deal of passive, intimate reproach latent in her, where he was concerned, but no really objective hostility. He took a chance and told her. "I've got a furnished room around the corner from here, on Tillary Street."

"Well, get back there, for heaven's sake! Look, the crowd's starting to break up. Mingle in with them and you can make it. I'll go up and get my things, and then I'll slip over there after you."

"I'll wait for you right here," he suggested.

She wouldn't hear of it. "No! No, Danny, I'm afraid! Please get back where you belong. It's just begging for something to happen to you if you hang around like this."

He gave a hitch of his head toward the underside of the staircase. "Who's up there?" he said. Even if he was supposed to know what the place was, whom it belonged to, and what she was doing up there, the question was still valid. Maybe she lived up there herself. In that case there was a short cut to finding out—no, on second thought, he'd found time to notice that there weren't even any downstairs doorbells out at the entrance there, much less names of tenants listed, so that wouldn't give him any clue to her identity.

Her answer wasn't particularly enlightening, except that it indicated he was supposed to know what the place was. "The whole darn bunch, and the family cat thrown in! It'll take me a few minutes to break away; I don't want them to tumble to anything. I'll tell them I'm taking an earlier train. You *can't* wait down here all that time."

Just the same, if there was going to be treachery, he was giving her a big, wide opening to get it in. There was no way of avoiding that, under the circumstances, he supposed. It would simply have to be risked. "All right," he agreed. "It's Number Fifteen, the second-floor front."

"Danny, *be* there now. Don't run out on me again." She half tilted her face with an air of expectancy. He brushed his lips past hers, rather than be guilty of an overt omission.

There had evidently been more wholehearted kiss-es exchanged between them in the past. "Don't overtax your strength," she commented sulkily. And then with more immediate urgency, as he drew away, "Danny, be careful getting back." She detained him a moment longer. "Keep your hat down more in front." Gave the brim a protective tug. Then let him go.

He went down the passage toward the street door. Behind him he heard the light tap of her climb on the stairs.

Who was she? What was she? She was obviously aware of his crime, but did she have any direct connection with it herself, or had she simply learned of it through his telling her?

Question marks, question marks, nothing but question marks. They kept popping up in his mind like dollar signs in a cash register.

He turned the corner into Tillary Street—not without a fleeting look back at the house that held her—and covered the short remaining distance back to his own room. His walk was brisk, purposeful, for the first time on Tillary Street. He overtook, made his way around, and past those who blocked him, charted a swift course. No more dilly-dallying along the sidewalks, that much at least was over. Tillary Street couldn't have anything more than this to give him. He had hoped to extract a chance nod, a casual word in passing. He had achieved tears of reproach, a slap across the mouth, a kiss of unrequited affection.

The payoff had been delayed, but it had been well worth waiting for.

11

It had been dark for hours. He'd had the gas jet lit long ago—
that was the most he could do for her in the way of hospitality—
and it was dancing impatiently, halfway up the wall, waiting for
her, a yellow angel on the head of a pin. And still she didn't show
up. It must be over three hours by now. No, four. Just around the
corner from here. What was this to be, another washout, another
false alarm? Or something even worse. Was a net, guided by her,
being carefully disposed around him; was that what was taking
so long? The only reason he didn't harbor this last thought with
any degree of consistency, but only at impatiently intermittent
intervals, was that it was taking too long even for treachery. The
whole thing would have been over by now, if that had been the
cause of delay. It was taking her too long for anything but just a
plain, old-fashioned stand-up.

He kept roaming back and forth, on the gently undulating
floor boards. He kept doing things that had no connection with
her expected arrival—turned the balky tap on, then off again—
to vary the unending monotony of doing the things that did:
peering out through the side gap of the shade at the street below, going over to the door, fanning it open (as though she were

a current of air and that would bring her into the room more quickly).

Intermittent suspicions, like fire tongues, darted their way up and down in his brain. How do I know who she is? I evidently did something to her, treated her shabbily in some way, in the past; how do I know what it was? Maybe if I knew, she'd be the last one I'd trust. Suppose she takes this chance of paying me back? She *seemed* all right, but women are unreliable that way. One minute they can be all forgiving, the next haul out a knife they've been carrying sheathed in their hearts for you. Or maybe it's just a mercenary angle, maybe there's a reward out for me, and she's around at the neighborhood precinct house right now, taking the first steps toward collect—

Wait a minute. Was that a rustle out there on the stairs? He took a quick, lithe, catlike jump over behind the door, bowed his head to chest level, ear close to the seam, hand pressed to the key against treacherous entry. A breath of silk came threading through the keyhole.

"Dan."

First he was going to open at demand. Then he thought: make her say her name. Take this opportunity to find out what it is. "Who is it?" he insisted in a low voice.

She got around that, probably without any conscious intent. "Me."

He made a grimace of wry disappointment to himself, turned the key.

She came in. Already a little spark of amber jealousy was glinting in her eyes. "You must be having quite a few girls up, if you have such a hard time telling them apart."

He closed the door, said something that was literally quite true—and he was afraid that many of the things he was going to have to say to her weren't going to be. "You're the first person that's come up, outside of the landlord, since I've been here."

"Don't make me laugh," was all the belief she gave him on this. "You'd never be lonely very long, no matter where you were. Don't I know you? Wait a minute, don't close the door. I've got my things out there."

She hauled in a small, battered suitcase, and two or three paper parcels.

Just what had they been to one another, anyway? He carefully ignored the name "Virginia" trying to form at the back of his mind. He watched her without a word.

"I can go straight from here to the train," she said. "In the morning. Take the six-o'clock one up there."

His mind asked: the six-o'clock one up *where?* His voice asked: "What time does that get you there?"

"Seven-ten," she said. And then, half rebukingly, "You ought to know that by now."

One hour and ten minutes away. One hour and ten minutes away from the city was a place marked X. But in which direction of the compass? There were so many to choose from. 180 degrees. Only one direction was excluded: south and its variants. That gave you the open sea.

He daren't ask the name of the place. But there was something he could ask that might help him to get it for himself, later, without her. He formulated a second question dealing with this train of hers; carefully reserved it in his mind for later. It couldn't be asked right now because there was no excuse for it; it would have been too glaringly disconnected. But when the right opportunity offered itself, he'd pop out with it.

She had been glancing around the room meanwhile. "Oh, Danny, this is a sha-ame."

He quirked one brow, implying, "What can you expect?"

She drew him closer under the sallow nimbus of the gas flame. "Let me look at you."

He let her, standing passive.

She traced the outline of his face, as though to get the "feel" of it. She didn't seem altogether satisfied. "Danny, there's something different about you. I wonder what it is?"

Townsend didn't risk an answer.

She sat down on the bed, still evidently missing some sort of harmony between them. He could tell that by the puzzled way she looked at him. "You sound so, sort of, cagey. What's happened to you, Danny? You act like you were afraid of saying the wrong thing."

I am, he thought. Oh, if you only knew how I am!

She opened the parcels she'd brought in, one by one. Groceries. A square object turned out to be a small gas burner. "I don't want you to have to budge out of here, from now on. You've got everything right here, there's nothing to take you on the street. You've got to quit taking crazy chances, like today. I want you to promise me you won't do that again."

She was bending down now, with her back to him, disposing the things along the baseboard of the wall, the only storage place in the room. Her shadow was cast on the wall before her. It loomed grim and ominous, like a prophet of doom. Then a horn squawked somewhere outside in the street and shattered the illusion.

She went on talking. "They never give up, don't forget that. When they seem to be laying low, that's when you've got to watch your step the most."

They. Who were *they?*

Her handbag lay on the bed, partly beneath him. There wasn't anything in it to tell him what he wanted to know. Surreptitiously he snapped the catch closed again. There was a vogue for big initials, but there were none on this bag. No short cuts in this, it seemed.

She came back, stretched out alongside him, began to play with the wing tip of his collar. "What're you going to do, Danny? Have you thought?"

"I wish I knew," he answered, carefully evasive.

"It's a losing game, isn't it? Why didn't you think of that before?"

"There's no jackpot in it." You could say that about anything, so it was safe enough to say it now.

She gave a mournful little laugh. "For me there isn't, that's a cinch." Her head sloped forward. Her cheek came to rest upon his chest. Her hair was like a soft, ruffled carpet under his chin. He stared out thoughtfully above her, listening to what she said. "It's funny, though. I wouldn't change places with any girl who has her fellow forever. Who knows no one's going to come and take him away from her any week, any day, any minute. I'd rather have you, Danny, than anyone else, even if I know I'm going to lose you one of these nights. Come around here and knock on the door, and no more Danny."

"No—no—" he drawled reassuringly, "we'll find a way." He knew he mustn't jolt her out of this kind of talk, with its infinite promise of revelation.

"I wonder if they smelled a rat over *there*," was the next thing she said.

The way she emphasized the adverb, he knew it was some place close by. The Watt Street flat, therefore, he supplied with a fair degree of certainty.

"Do you think they did?"

"I don't know," she said dubiously, "I don't know. Luckily my sister was in the kitchen giving one of the kids a bath, when I hollered out your name that time. I could have bitten my tongue off a minute later. But it popped out before I could stop it."

Her sister's flat, then. Her married sister's flat. She was visiting it from one hour and ten minutes away—in some one of one hundred and eighty approximate directions.

"She couldn't leave the kid even to watch the fire. But when I came back upstairs again later she said, 'Didn't I hear you holler out Dan a little while ago?' and gave me kind of a suspicious squint. I laughed and covered it up the best way I could. I told her that I hollered 'Scram!' to some kids that was teasing a dog."

She waited a minute, then added apprehensively, "I only hope she believed me."

The conversation showed signs of lagging. She stirred a little. "It must be getting late. I don't want to miss my train in the morning."

He stretched his arm up overhead, along the wall behind them, turned the key on the gas jet. Nothing was left but that ghost window thrown upward from the street. Just that, and the murmur of their two voices, even lower now than before. Her mention of the train was the opening he'd been hoping and waiting for all along, the opening for that second question, held carefully in reserve until now.

"What track does it leave on?" he asked, as casually as he could.

He got a rebuke on it again, but he also got what he was after. "You ought to know, you took enough of those trains yourself. They all leave from the same track. Seventeen, lower level."

To get the answer to any given equation, you need at least

two of its component parts. He had them both now. One hour and ten minutes away. Track seventeen, lower level, six A. M. That would give the name of the place.

She had put tracks and trains out of her mind now. Out of both their minds.

"You kiss me like you were thinking of something else."

Well as a matter of fact, he had kissed her from one hour and ten minutes away. He brought his thoughts back, kissed her again. "What's the matter with that one?"

"The mere fact that you've got to give out a testimonial with it."

He was wondering how he could find out her name. In almost every phrase he addressed to her, there was an awkward letdown at the end, where her name should have rounded it out. The tongue expected it. The ear expected it, too.

He rigged up a little trap, to see if he could snare it out of her. It was one of those questions that blended in perfectly with the circumstances of the moment. His voice was low, beside her ear. "If you could change your name, what would you rather have it be?"

It got him a name—his own, not hers. "That's a pushover, Mrs. Daniel Nearing."

He said it over to himself. Dan Nearing. Another key to the past.

He took a chance, suggested: "That would make it longer than it is now." Nearing was a fairly short name.

She had to figure it aloud, as he'd hoped she would. "Only one letter. Let's see. D-i-l-l-o-n, six. N-e-a-r-i-n-g, seven." Then with a little burst of petulance, "Say, what is this anyway, a spelling bee in the dark?"

"I was just talking," he tried to pacify her. "You know how it is—it's been a long time since we talked together. I like to talk to you."

"Sure, talking's all right," she agreed sulkily, "but there are other things besides conversation."

He didn't say anything more for a while. "How's this, for not conversing?" he asked her presently.

"For my part, you should never say another word."

In the morning he found his arm curved around nothing, giving emptiness a hug where she had been. But she'd be back again, the note said so.

> *Danny Darling, I had to make that six o'clock, and I didn't have the heart to wake you. Until next Thursday, and please be careful in the meantime.*
>
> RUTH

Her name was Ruth Dillon, the place she trained to and from was one hour and ten minutes away, the train that took her there left on Track 17 lower level—and he felt as if he'd been pulled through a wringer.

12

HE KNEW he was taking a chance. Stations are dangerous places to frequent, for those in hiding.

He came down the broad stairs from the upper level, chin ducked to shirt front, to conceal at least the lower part of his face. It was about the safest hour he could have picked, five forty-five A. M. The huge place was at its emptiest; there was less chance of unfriendly eyes spotting him than at almost any other time of the night or day. Conversely, his peril was increased by that very fact. He was conspicuous; there wasn't any crowd to blend in with; it was like being alone on a vast stage. You're bound to attract whatever eyes there are.

He was here at the exact hour of her departure the day before, because that was the only way to make sure the train going out now on 17 would have an identical schedule to hers.

There were a handful of forlorn, sleepy-looking travelers scattered about on the benches, idle redcap or two hanging about. Since he wasn't carrying anything, they didn't approach him.

He worked his way back along the gates, from the high numbers to the low. 23, 21, 19. There it was, 17, with the schedule of its next departure conveniently posted up alongside it. He sidled onto a bench opposite it, and studied the list of stops. No arrival hours were given, only the time of departure from here, 6 A. M., so he saw he'd have to work it out by a process of elimination.

He looked guardedly around, and when the entire marble floor of the huge place was at its clearest, no one crossing it, he got up again and went over to the gateman. He picked a name at random from the board, the exact middle one, the halfway point of the trip.

"What time does this train get to Clayburgh?"

"Six fifty-five."

A quarter of an hour too near. He dropped down to the next one.

"What time does it hit Meredith?"

"Seven-five."

Not it yet. It must be the next one.

"How about New Jericho?"

The gateman was getting restive. "Seven-ten," he said gruffly. His look said, "How much longer you going to keep this up?"

Townsend was through. He turned away. He'd hit the place. New Jericho was where she came and went from.

He was one step farther on the way. Now he must get out of here again as safely as he'd come in—

13

THURSDAY AGAIN. Two voices in the dark again. The game of love and tightrope walking again.

He'd charted his course ahead of time, before she came. The things he'd found out filled him with an insatiable passion to lift the curtain higher. He was like a man who has taken a long, tranquil voyage, and finds himself mad with impatience during the last hour before he will be home again.

There were two main things to be elicited tonight. Two things that must be kept in sight, like twin lanterns far down a tunnel, no matter what tortuous passages they went through. *Where* had it happened? *When* had it happened?

The place. The date. Then he could go on from there. Those were the two factors of the equation he needed, Once he had them, he could work out the answer. He must get them.

Even as his lips touched hers, his mind kept ticking off: *where and when? Where and when?*

She got up, crossed the room to lower the shade.

Where and when? Where and when? Where and when?

When she came back, she hesitated a moment before rejoining him. As though some spark of resentment had fanned itself alight within her, during her brief absence. He could tell. Couples are almost telepathic at such times.

"What're you sore about?" he murmured in the dark.

"Who's Virginia?"

He swallowed, unseen. "I don't know. Where'd you get that name from?"

"From you."

"You're hearing things."

Where, and when? Where, and when? Where, and when?

"Somebody you horsed around with up at New Jericho?" she went on resentfully. "Or is it somebody you dug up for yourself since you been hiding out down here in the city?"

"I've been undercover the whole time down here—"

"Well you weren't undercover up there!" she flashed back.

That gave him the answer. The one answer he had already guessed. Up there was *where*. New Jericho. Only one remaining lantern to steer for now. When? When? When?

Meanwhile she was still aggrieved. "Let her buy your groceries for you, then, if she's so hot! That's a fine thing! I've got to hear somebody else's name in my ear, even—"

"Sh! they'll hear you around this dump. Listen, there's no Virginia. I don't know any Virginia. To me it's a state—"

"*You* weren't thinking of geography just then!" she let him know seethingly.

He reached out and caught hold of her hand. She came back to him by diminishing zones of aloofness. First sitting stiffly on the edge of the bed, her back to him. Then reclining on the point of one elbow, face still averted. Then relapsing in full forgiveness, head to his shoulder once more.

When? When? When?

"Light one for me too. Like you used to. . . . Gee your eyes look shiny by matchlight, Danny. . . . No, don't blow it out! Save it for me, I want to make a wish. . . . There. . . . What was it? You ought to be able to guess. That they'll never catch up with you; that they'll let me keep you to myself like this, forever."

Forever. A time word. There it was, right there. Better grab it quick, he mightn't get another chance that night.

"Forever is a long time. How long has it been   like this with me now? Any idea? I'm not so good at keeping track of time—"

"Nine months now, isn't it?" The question tricked her into some more of that audible counting up that is a weakness of those who are imperfectly schooled. "Let's see, August, September, October . . . yeah, it was nine months on the fifteenth. I don't know how you've been able to hold out that long—"

So it had happened, whatever it was, on August fifteenth, the year before.

Where, plus when, equals the past.

14

HE WAS as timorous about entering the reading room of the library as he had been of venturing into the station, although it had a reassuring atmosphere of scholarly absorption, of seclusion from the everyday world. Still, who could tell what eyes might not suddenly look up, rest on him in explosive recognition?

He kept his head down as he approached the reservation desk, got in line behind several others.

"Do you keep any back numbers of newspapers from New Jericho on file here?"

The attendant looked it up for him. "No, I'm sorry, we don't."

Maybe none were published there. Who could tell how small a place it was? It might be just an unincorporated crossroads.

He tried another question. "Have you any idea, offhand, what the nearest large town to it is?"

The librarian didn't seem surprised, as though this was less erratic than many another question he had been called upon to answer in his time. "I'm not sure, but I believe Meredith would be about the closest."

"Well, have you any Meredith back-number papers on file here?"

The attendant looked that up. "We have the Meredith *Leader,* but I don't know how complete a file we have on it. Fill out this card and then wait over there by the call board until your number comes up."

He filled it out "Meredith *Leader,* August 16th, 1940," and signed it "Allen." That would be about right, the day after.

When the paper was brought to him he handled it gingerly. Suddenly he wanted to drop it, never to look inside it. He wanted to escape from this room, from Tillary Street, from himself. The past was here in his hands, and he was afraid of it. Frank Townsend and Dan Nearing were together at last.

What had Dan Nearing done? He took the paper over with him to one of the tables and sat down in front of it with desperate resignation. He opened the paper.

The name "Dan Nearing" leaped out at him. He huddled forward, began to read within a sort of protective barricade formed by his extended arms.

KILLS BENEFACTOR

Brutal Slaying at Suburban Estate

New Jericho, *Aug. 15th*—Turning on the man who had given him shelter and employment during the past two years, Daniel Nearing shot and killed Harry S. Diedrich, member of a well-known local family, at his country home near here early yesterday afternoon. The victim's wife, Alma, his younger brother, William, and a neighbor, Arthur Struthers, were horrified eyewitnesses to the crime, having returned unexpectedly for a book of commutation tickets they had overlooked on leaving a few moments before. They narrowly escaped sharing Mr. Diedrich's fate. The enraged assailant pursued them from the house when he caught sight of them. They managed to regain the highway in their car and telephone for help from Mr. Struthers' house. By the time police, under the direction of Constable E. J. Ames, had reached the scene, the slayer had made good his escape. The weapon used, a shotgun, was found lying where the killer had discarded it. The slain man's father, Emil Diedrich, a helpless invalid, was found unharmed in his wheel chair in another room of the house.

Nearing, whose antecedents are unknown, had been taken in and given work by the murdered man against the advice of other members of the household. Originally he worked as handy man about the premises, engaged to look after the grounds. For the past few months, however, he had been placed in charge of Mr. Diedrich's invalid father and had occupied a room within the house itself, replacing a former attendant who had been dismissed.

Other members of the household, at the time of the tragedy, consisted of Mr. Diedrich's sister, Adela, secluded in an upstairs room due to a nervous disorder, a cook, Mrs. Mollie McGuire, and a housemaid, Miss Ruth Dillon. The two servants were not present at the time of the tragedy, having left shortly before on their afternoon off.

According to the story pieced together by Constable Ames, Mrs. Diedrich during luncheon had expressed a wish to go to the city on a shopping trip. Her husband suggested that his brother drive her in to New Jericho to take the train. They set out shortly before two for the drive to the station. Mr. Diedrich, meanwhile, had retired to a

conservatory at the side of the house where he habitual-
ly took an afternoon nap. Mrs. McGuire and Miss Dillon left within a few moments after that, and took the bus
together. Nearing, when last seen, was sitting beside his
charge, apparently dozing.

Mrs. Diedrich and her brother-in-law, on their way to
the station, encountered Mr. Struthers, whom they knew
by sight, and offered to take him in with them. A moment
later Mrs. Diedrich discovered she had mislaid her train
tickets, and they turned back to enable her to get them. As
they drove up before the house, a gunshot sounded from
the conservatory. Before they could get out of the car,
Nearing had come rushing out of the conservatory bran-
dishing the still-smoking shotgun. Horrified, they drove
down to the highway again, pursued by him.

Mr. Diedrich, when the police arrived on the scene,
was found to have been killed instantly. The victim's head
had been partly blown off by the blast. A small safe in the
library near by was discovered forced open, with its con-
tents scattered about on the floor. Whether any money
was missing could not immediately be learned. Mr Diedrich had complained of missing small sums in cash from
time to time over a period of several weeks past, and the
police are inclined to the belief that he set a trap for the
thief, discovered Nearing in the act of ransacking the safe,
attempted to call for help, and was driven back into the
conservatory by the enraged malefactor at the point of the
gun and there shot to death.

According to the description furnished Ames, the killer is of medium height, about twenty-seven or -eight years

of age, with light-brown hair and eyes, and with a deceptively mild appearance. He has a small blue anchor tattooed on the back of his left wrist.

The police are watching all main roads leading into the city, and an arrest is expected momentarily.

He let his cuff slide forward again, and the little blue anchor ebbed from sight under it.

Murder! It lit up his mind like a rocket. One of those flashing things that hang suspended against the night at a fireworks display and light up everything a pale, ghastly green.

He brushed the back of his hand across his mouth, as if to wipe off some sort of foul taste. He was one of *them* now. He could be hunted down. He could be killed by law. He was a murderer.

There was no refuge for him, no mercy. Earthly laws only fulfilled what divine law itself sanctioned. "Whoso sheddeth man's blood, by man shall his blood be shed."

He was a murderer. Outcast, taboo.

Now he knew, now he understood; the meaning of the man in gray, the silent grim pursuit, that raid in the dead of night on his home. Now the curtain had lifted and he saw what lay before him. No personal vengeance, no private enemy stalking him from out the miasmas of the past. That had been organized society itself. That man must have been of the police. Who else would have dared draw a gun on a crowded subway platform and shatter a car panel?

A hand fell on him lightly, and the touch of it went to his heart like electricity. "No sleeping in here, please," a voice murmured tactfully.

He raised his head again from between his arms. His eyes

were haunted. He'd been watching a man—twenty-seven or twenty-eight, light-brown hair and eyes, medium height—come rushing out of an enclosed room, holding a smoking shotgun in his hands.

15

THERE WAS a difference now. They weren't alone any more. There was a ghost there in the room with them. In the very bed with them. No matter how close he pulled her to him, it was still in the way. And when he tried to kiss her, he was kissing its cold, grinning face instead.

"Why are you so quiet tonight? What's the matter, Danny?"

He knew he had to do one of two things. Go up the steps into some building with green lamps at its entrance and say, "I'm Dan Nearing." Or—

He couldn't live with the thought any more.

"Ruth, do *you* believe I did that? You know."

She hid her face against him. "Three people saw you with their own eyes. I've *tried* not to—"

"But if I said I didn't, would you still believe I did?"

"Gee, I'd try harder than ever not to. I don't know if I could or not."

"And if I said I didn't, would you try to help me prove I didn't? Would you try to help me find out who really did?"

"Oh, Danny, I'd do *anything!* But how? What're you going to do?"

"I'm going back there. Right back where it happened. That's the only way to prove it. And you've got to help me."

She left his arms, and even the bed, almost in one unbroken, streamlined bound. She stood there aghast, before him in the dark. Her voice was a pin-stuck squeak. "To New Jericho? To the Diedrich place? D'you know what they'll *do?* No, Danny! Don't—*please!* For me. Stay here, where at least you've got a chance."

"I've got to. That's just it. I *have* no chance while I stay here. It's up there that my only chance is."

"But, Danny, it'll be like sticking your head into a trap. They'll turn you in so fast—"

"*If* they see me," he said doggedly. "That's where you come in."

"Danny," she faltered, "it can't be done; we'd never get away with it—"

He cut her short. "I've been thinking it over for days, and my mind's made up. If you don't help me, then I'm going anyway, on my own. It'll be just that much tougher. *I know I didn't do that.* Don't ask me to back that up. I can't. I know three people saw me. I know it's in the papers, and on the cops' blotters. I don't care. I don't care if the whole world says I killed that man. *I* say I didn't. The *me* that's in me says I didn't! I won't lie down and let them tell me different. Not while there's a breath left in me. I won't lie down and take it. I'm going back. It's going to end where it began. One way or the other. Now are you with me or against me? Are you on my side or on theirs? Will you help me or will you let me go hang?"

She bent down toward him in the dark. Her hair swept forward, rippling over his shoulders like soft, warm rain. Her lips sought his, and just before they met, in a kiss that was a pledge, she murmured: "You don't have to ask me that. Don't you know I'd help you, Danny, even if it was the last thing I ever did!"

BOOK III

Behind the Curtain

16

THIS WAS the night set for his return to yesterday. The last train out, at eleven. All the necessary details had been arranged between them on her last visit, the week before. She was to bring in some clothes for him to put on, to alter his appearance as much as possible. She was to come straight to the room, from the station. Up *there,* she had remembered, there was a sort of disused lodge or cabin. Nobody ever went near it. It would do to conceal his presence.

Darkness had fallen on Tillary Street, and for the last time the lambent ghost embrasure flickered on the room wall. It seemed, while he waited and she became longer and longer overdue, to mock at him, as if it were saying: "You'll never make it. You'll never get out of here."

He couldn't stand it finally, and badly as he wanted to watch for her from the window he jerked down the shade to kill the blasted mirage. Of a window where there was no window. Of a way out where there was none.

But that didn't bring her any faster. He craned his neck, peering out through the side of the shade, until it ached from the distorted position. The sidewalk crowd below seemed to be toiling up and down a ramp that descended toward his vantage point.

She should have reached the city hours ago. She had said she would join him by midafternoon at the latest, even though, for safety's sake, they weren't going to try to start back until the last train.

He needed her more than she realized. She thought he'd been up there before. His body had, but his mind hadn't. He couldn't move an inch without her. He was as helpless as a blind man trying to cross a street without a guide. He couldn't make it without her.

And she wasn't coming any more, you could tell that. She would have been here by now. She'd let him down, not purposely, but that didn't help. He knew now there was no question of treachery, of disloyalty, involved. She was all for him, as much as Virginia herself could have been if she'd been called on to play this part. Some unforeseen slip-up must have occurred. Maybe she'd broken a leg up there, groping her way around the littered interior of that shack, trying to get it ready for him. Maybe there'd been a tie-up of train service on the way down. But even so, four or five hours was a pretty long time for anything of that sort to last. Maybe she'd reached the city safely and then been run down in the streets on her way down here to him. She might be laid up helpless right now in the accident ward of one of the hospitals.

There came that chime again, from some buried little steeple hiding among the tenements. He counted it, although he knew what it was going to add up to.

Clongg, Clongg, Clongg—eight, nine, ten. Just one hour left. Enough time, if he left almost at once, to get that train. The point was, if she hadn't come by now, there was no use counting on her, she wasn't coming at all any more. What was he going to do then? Stay and rot here for another week? She mightn't come next week either. For all he knew, *he might never see her again.*

How could he make it without her? How could he possibly hope to run the gantlet of recognition? They must know him so well, up there at the other end. The very first person he approached to ask directions—and he would have to ask directions—might turn him in. Even walking around down here in the city was risky. That was why she'd been bringing in concealing clothes for him. Railway stations were the worst places for him; brightly lighted, always alive with *them,* on the lookout for people trying to escape. They couldn't know that he was trying to return to the past. You had to file in through narrow, easily watched gates to get to the trains.

To tackle the undertaking, alone and unaided, was more than inviting arrest, it was *making certain* of it. But—

He was going to do it.

He couldn't put on a wig or dye his face, but there must be something he could do, to give himself a fighting chance to pass unnoticed. Wait a minute, that old furrier down on the ground floor. The one that salvaged scraps of worn-out, discarded fur and matched them together with shears and glue and then went peddling them around among the neighborhood drudges at fifty cents and a dollar a throw.

A moment later he was looking in at him through the open door, the door always left open because of the smell of the glue he used in his work. "Listen, I want to play a trick on my girl. You know, just for fun. Put me a dab of glue here, on each side, just in front of my ears. And one on each eyebrow. Then take a few thin pieces of dark fur, the ends you don't need, and see if you can make them look like they were growing there."

The fur repairer waved outraged arms. "Funny business I got no time to make."

"Here's a quarter. Listen, you're good at that, you can do it."

The peddler sounded the quarter against the bare floor board, then accommodatingly poised an agglutinated brush toward Townsend's face. "The way this glue makes you smell, your girl ain't going to like you so much," he warned.

It took them too much time to get a halfway naturalistic effect. His hat, pulled down low so that only the thinned-out sealskin sideburns and eyebrows showed beneath it, took away a good deal of the curse. His coat collar, upped in back, covered the neck hair. He'd even tried out a few strands against his upper lip, but that was no good, had to be discarded.

It was the most he could do for himself, and it was little enough. Anyone that already knew him would know him at once. This was just for those who mightn't be sure at first sight. This was just his fighting chance, in a crowd, with luck.

He went back to his room again for a minute, hoping against hope she'd still come, even this late. The room was empty. He'd have to strike out on his own.

He took a deep breath, rubbed himself briskly down both arms at once. "Well—here goes." He reached up and tweaked out the gas cockade pinned onto the jet.

Tillary Street sank from sight, returned into that past from which he'd so patiently dredged it.

17

A RETRIEVED newspaper, held spread out inches away from his eyes throughout the subway trip, had helped. But he couldn't hold it in that position on his way to and from his seat, and it was in those brief exposed passages that the danger lay. Having to walk between those two endless-seeming rows of upturned, idly-inspecting faces. But nothing had happened. Doom must have been pulling its punches, saving them for the rounds ahead.

Now the station, gained by underground causeway, a lesser risk than the streets above. As he came out into the vast expanse of the main waiting room, the symptoms of agoraphobia struck him full blast. He felt as though the walls were a thousand miles away from him on all sides. He felt as though he were walking alone, with not another moving object to mar his conspicuousness, across this immense expanse of marble and cement. He felt as though a spotlight were focused squarely on him from head to toe, following him across this tremendous amphitheater every step of the way, with nothing to hide behind, nothing to break the *openness*. And all around him, unseen, in a hideous circular line-up, faces scanning, scrutinizing, staring at him.

He got over to a ticket window, saw that it was the wrong one. Moved on to another. "Gimme a ticket to New Jericho."

"Dollar eighty-four."

He kept looking around while he scooped money out of his pocket.

But the ticket seller kept the pad of his finger pressed down on the oblong stub, even after Townsend had thrust every coin in his pocket across the slab. "You're a penny short. Dollar eighty four."

"That's all I have on me. I must have miscounted. Can't you—?"

"I can't sell you a ticket unless you give me the exact amount for it."

"But it's only a *cent*. Only a penny. That can't hurt. I'm not trying to do this purposely—" That damned eyebrow stunt was to blame for this! He would have had twenty-four cents over what he needed if it hadn't been for that.

"D'you know I can lose my job if I sell you a ticket for less than the amount stamped on the face of it?" Maybe he was new at the job. Maybe they really weren't supposed to.

Already somebody had come up, was standing behind him on line, getting a beautiful chance to study him at leisure. "Listen, don't make me lose that train, will you, all over a penny! It's two to, now!"

The ticket seller had hard crullers of stubbornness around his eyes. "The full amount of every ticket I give out has to come back to me through this window. I don't care if it's a penny or what it is! What do you expect me to do, shell out of my own pocket for *you?*" Townsend saw him turn aside and spear the thing back into the rack he'd pulled it out of.

The man behind jostled him slightly, and suddenly he found himself too far forward past the wicket to continue arguing. He turned and shuffled off, hugging the line of ticket windows closely. A break came in them, and he glimpsed a smaller, pocket-sized waiting room, tiered with benches. He slunk in there. Anything to get out of that big, open rotunda. Anything to get away from his own desperate helplessness.

He sidled around the outside perimeter of the place, trying to get to the farthest back of all the rows of benches, to sit the night out and wait for—nothing.

There was a man standing in his way, shaking or worrying at something. Somebody else's voice said, "Come on, we haven't time!" and the man thrust hurriedly by him. That cleared a narrow strip of mirror, in which Townsend saw his own reflection. He stopped and eyed it, as though seeing a stranger. He looked with impersonal interest at the subterfuge eyebrows. Below the mirror, one of the three rods that operated the slot machine was held back at quarter length, caught fast in some way. It had no definite meaning to him. He hit it instinctively, trying to make it even.

The rod ricocheted to its full length. A penny, a very black and time-worn Indian head, clicked down the little chute where packaged gum should have issued.

He turned and fled back to the ticket window with it, at forty-five seconds to eleven.

Hatred was still at red heat between them. "Here's your penny, you son of a bitch!" Townsend said bitterly.

"And here's your ticket, you bastard!" the man behind the grille flared back at him.

He squeezed through the gate just as they were closing it. He careened down the ramp and caught hold of a vestibule handle bar just as motion had set in. The conductor reopened the door and let him in.

It was the last train of the night, and it was full. He treaded through the car he'd boarded, and there wasn't a seat to be had. He kept moving toward the locomotive, trying to find a place to sink down in out of sight. In the third car up he nearly blundered into catastrophe.

Two things saved him. Two more of those trifling variations which had so consistently saved him.

The chair backs of these day coaches operated on the swivel principle, could be faced whichever way the train was going. All but one of them in the whole car, on both sides of the aisle, was facing forward. *All but one.* Either it had jammed or else had been purposely turned that way by its occupant, so that he could converse more conveniently face to face with the two people opposite him.

The second miracle was that the occupant of the fourth seat provided by this double arrangement was Ruth Dillon. Perhaps she had had difficulty in finding a seat and had taken what she could get, even if it meant riding backwards. She, and the stranger next to her, busily talking to his friends opposite, were the only two people in the entire car facing Townsend; in a position to see him before he blundered on past them into irretrievable exposure.

She knew him instantly (proving what a waste of time and effort the fur-bearing eyebrows had been). Her eyes dilated with horror, then quickly contracted again—not because horror was any the less but because they dare not betray themselves by protracted staring.

Luckily he'd fallen motionless in mid-footfall, the aisle

door just newly closed at his back. She had time to do only two things, and they were so slight that the very act of continuing motion might have lost them to his sight. She made a fleeting, warding-off gesture with her palms that for him could have only one meaning: "Don't come in here. Don't come near me." Then she deflected her eyes toward the aisle, swiftly, urgently. To Townsend the message was clear. She was trying to say, "Look behind me. Look up the aisle."

He did. Two seats past her, on the opposite side, was that same outline of side face and shoulder, under the same gray hat, that had hunted him in another life. A tensing of the man's neck cords indicated that his head was about to swing around. Either to make sure Ruth was still safely where his last look had placed her, or because the opening and closing of the car door just now was about to draw a belated glance from him.

A pace farther forward into the car and Townsend couldn't have made it. Even so, with the door at his very back, he couldn't get out again. The upper half was glass and the oncoming look would have skewered him through it before he could move out of the way. He shouldered open the panel beside him and was gone. The closing of the washroom door must have synchronized with the completion of that head turn. It left nothing to see but vacant space.

He rode the rest of the way, out of one state and into the next, in uncomfortable perpendicular confinement, back to door, one leg up against the opposite wall to brace himself. He counted five stops and three unsuccessful door tries. The ease with which they were discouraged showed, at least, that they weren't made by his nemesis in the gray suit out there. But the mere fact that a number of people were denied admittance might bring about a shattering investigation.

He perspired profusely in there. For the first time he had completely lost all freedom of movement. He hadn't even been this closely trapped the night they had broken into the Anderson Avenue flat; at least there had been a dumbwaiter and a basement there. He wouldn't know which stop it was now, either. Certainly not in time to get off. The sliver of window was slightly open at the top, but it was fixed fast and the glass was opaque. The strangled station calls of the conductor, behind him in the car, didn't penetrate here at all. And if he rode too far past the mileage value of his ticket, he was running the risk of detention by the trainmen, when he came out, on charges of trying to beat his way, with all the attendant consequences of revelation of identity. The whole thing depended on whether that professionally alert individual out there happened to notice, after a while, that a usually accessible door had suddenly closed for business for the entire duration of the trip.

The sudden motionlessness of the sixth stop was followed, after the briefest of intervals, by a glancing impact, a sort of scuff, down near the bottom of the door. Its repetition, in a matter of seconds, showed it to be a signal, no carelessness of tread on the part of someone going by. She must have found time to do it on her way past, perhaps backwards, with the heel of her shoe.

He opened instantly. She had lingered there, back to him, pretending to powder her nose. She didn't turn, spoke to him into the pocket mirror she was using. "Ames," she breathed hurriedly. "He got off at the other end of the car just now, to try to keep out of my sight. He's out there on the station some place. Count ten, slowly, from the time I leave the bottom step—then swing off yourself. Now listen closely. We only have about a minute and a half. There's a baggage truck piled up with trunks standing over there against the station wall, right near us, just a little way down that way. I can see it from here through the car window. Get over to it, and get behind it, and don't move. I think I can work it. If I can't come near you right away, I'll come back for you later, as soon as I'm sure I've shaken him off. Wait for me there, don't go away. Remember, ten, slowly."

He came out into the aisle just as her figure disappeared around the turn of the vestibule. He heard the click of her descending heels on the steel-rimmed car steps. He started the count she'd arranged with him. One . . . two . . . three . . .

"'Boooard!" echoed dismally outside on the platform.

The train was moving by the time he hit ten. He'd have to go *back* now, to get in behind the hand truck, not forward; it had already slipped past to the other side of the door. Just as he broke shelter past the car door a wailing scream wrenched from her, somewhere farther back toward the passenger exit. It was a slick piece of timing.

He had sense enough to keep going straight for the shelter with a grim economy of direction, but he couldn't help glimpsing the vignette she had artfully produced down there.

Every head along the platform had turned her way. A pretty girl turning her foot like that and floundering down on one hand and knee, with a scream to advertise it, couldn't help but monopolize every eye—even a detective's. From behind the backed-up truck Townsend could see a small knot of people gather around her, help her up, dust her off, and sympathize with her. Then they straggled off at one end while the hum of the train receded at the other. The long concrete platform fell silent and empty under its piebald black and white markings of wide-spaced arclights and intervening shadow troughs.

The six-eight time of her heel taps, coming back again a good quarter of an hour later, was the first sound to break it in all that time. Local stations like this were lifeless except at the actual moments of train arrival.

He looked out from his niche as she reached him. "All right now?"

"All right now. I stopped in at Jordan's drugstore across the square and had a spot of iodine put on the palm of my hand. I had to have an excuse to hang around, so I had a soda at the counter. He went straight into the constable's office; I saw him through the drugstore window. That's one good thing about these hick towns that have just one main street; you can spot everything that's going on."

"How do you know he's gone off duty? Isn't he liable to be still watching you?"

"Not once I'm back here any more. He's not interested in me out here, where I work and sleep seven days a week. It was only in the city that he kept breathing down the back of my neck. Probably the only reason he got on the same train coming back was there isn't any other until 6 A. M. What a day he gave me, though! And talk about close shaves! I just about avoided giving myself away by the skin of my teeth. Another minute and I wouldn't have known he was tailing me and would have led him straight down into your lap! I'm telling you, Dan, I already had one foot raised to the bus step, to take me down to Tillary Street, when I saw him." She sighed with remembered fright. "Lucky he didn't catch on that I saw him. Well, I went ahead and got right on that same bus, as though I hadn't seen a thing. But was I icicles in the feet!"

He gave her a questioning look.

"I had to. I couldn't have backed out, once he'd seen me on the point of getting in the first time. He would have caught on in a minute I was trying to throw him off the scent, and that was the one thing I didn't want him to think. Don't you see, you take the same bus line for Watt Street that you would for Tillary Street, what's the difference? But what counted was I knew now that every move I made was being watched. So I got off at my sister's and spent the afternoon there and had supper with them. I made my brother-in-law a present of the things in the bag, told him I'd brought them in specially for him. That covered that. And d'you know where I was all evening, until half an hour before traintime? At Loew's. I had to go *somewhere,* and keep as far away from you as possible. I knew I daren't even try to go near you any more for the rest of the day or night. I couldn't take the chance."

Townsend said, "That was smart work, Ruth."

She flushed at his tribute, went on. "You can imagine how I felt; I had to sit looking at Cesar Romero, and all I could see was your face in front of me the whole time, waiting down there. Ames was probably somewhere in the audience through the whole show, but he didn't slip up a second time. I never saw him again after that, from the time I got on the bus, until I came through the cars looking for a seat on the train coming home. That's harder even than to follow someone: to *let* yourself be followed without letting on you know it's being done."

Townsend said, "What does he want with you?"

"It's on account of you, of course. He must have a hunch I've been seeing you. God knows why! Don't let anyone tell you they're not *good.* They're *good* all right. They're mind readers and magicians all rolled up in one."

"No they're not," he scoffed. "They're just plain this." He snapped his fingernail at the back of his own hand, made the skin quiver. "They can be wrong, too. They think I killed Diedrich. I say I didn't."

"And if you say that, I say that, too. Now the thing is, how're we going to get you away from here and out there?"

"How do you usually go yourself?"

"I take the bus from the square here, it brings me right out to the door. But that's out, for you." She looked around, in search of inspiration. "Wait a minute, I just happened to notice something when I came back for you. There's a truck standing out front, the other side of the station. The drivers must be in Joe's Lunch getting a meal. If I can find out whether it's going the right way for us, we wouldn't have to be afraid to ask them to give us a lift. They wouldn't know us. They're not from around here, just passing through. Come on around the outside of the station, don't pass through the waiting room. The agent's gone off duty, but there's still a porter somewhere around."

He followed her around the upper end of the neat little one-story concrete building. She stopped and pointed. "See it? Just down there? That's the one I meant."

He squeezed her arm admiringly. "You see everything."

"You have to, when you're looking out for someone you love." She said it with the utmost simplicity. "There they are, coming out now. Stay here close under the shed until I find out. If it's O.K. I'll wave you on. Cut straight over to it fast, don't stay out in the open any longer than you have to. Ames will probably still be in there half the night making out his report, but still you never know—"

He watched her go over, stand there a moment talking to one of the two drivers. He saw the fellow touch his cap to her. Then he saw one white-gloved hand go up, in an overhand signal, through the intervening gloom.

He broke out, walked fast across the considerable exposed

space behind the station, talcumed with arclight, and got in again behind the welcome shadow cast by the bulky aluminum-faced truck.

"It's all right, *Jimmy*," she shrieked above the din of its warming-up motor. "These boys said they'll give us a lift out to where we work. I told them what happened to your wallet. You'll have to climb up into the back, there's only room for three on the front seat."

He pantomimed his thanks to their hosts by saluting toward one of the shadowy, aproned figures visible beside her, up there at the other end, without approaching any closer.

The rear apron had been left conveniently down; they were evidently making the return trip empty. He scrambled up onto it, shifted a little farther in, to where the body of the truck itself began, and propped himself up there with a neat triangle of shadow catching him protectively from the knees up.

They rumbled off and New Jericho village, hardly seen as yet, receded behind him in a blurred checkerboard of arclights and black squares. Then a long, tapelike country highway started to unroll behind him, with black tracery on both sides of it that were roadside trees, an occasional house, and pollen of stars up above.

A good thirty to forty minutes of that, without a break. Or so it seemed, though it may have been less. Once a passenger car, coming up from behind and overtaking them, gave him a few bad moments. Its heads hit a big yellow sphere against the inner wall of the truck opposite to where he was. The light started to creep over to his side, as the machine behind them shifted to go past on the outside. His legs were bathed in it, and it started to climb up him. He cocked his knees, thrust his head down between them, and wrapped his arms over it, as though he'd fallen asleep in a sitting position. The car swerved out and went past and he reared up again.

About five minutes after that the truck shuddered to a throbbing halt and Ruth's piercing tones filtered back to him above the engine drumbeat. "Thanks a lot, boys. You're lifesavers. *Jimmy*, you clear?"

He vaulted down off the apron, and a moment later he and she were standing all alone by the roadside in a little haze of gasoline exhaust. She pressed her hip joint, where it evidently ached from cramped sitting.

"My heart was in my mouth. Did you recognize who that was went by, awhile back?"

"I ducked my head."

"Bill and Alma Diedrich! I recognized the car. So that's what they've been doing, whenever I have a night off and they're supposed to stay home and keep an eye on the old man! Why, that's criminal, Dan! D'you know that there's not another living soul in the house with that helpless old man, except the crazy sister, Adela, and if she ever got out of her room there's no telling what she'd do to him. Anything could happen; a short-circuit could start a fire or—"

Maybe, he wondered to himself, they wouldn't be too sorry.

She pointed to a dimly discernible asphalted cutoff a short distance behind them. "That's the way I go in. Hurry up, let's get away from here before we're seen. We've still got a long walk ahead of us."

He couldn't help looking back in that direction, lingeringly. So that was the way in to murder. There was a white signboard swaying mid-center over it, strung from some invisible support. He imagined it would read: PRIVATE PROPERTY, NO THOROUGHFARE.

They crossed over but kept on along the roadside for a considerable distance, Indian file, she in the lead. "There's a much shorter way than this," she explained, "along a path that leads over to the shack from the house itself, but I don't want to bring you that near if I can help it. If they only just got back ahead of us, they might still be up, and one of them might see you from the windows."

The main driveway had long been just a memory behind them, and still she kept going ahead of him. If it was equal in depth to its parallel length along the highway, it was some private estate! A young county.

She stopped finally. "There's their boundary marker. See it up ahead there? That white circle painted around the trunk of the tree. We'll cut in through here now. There's just a short stretch before us where we'll have to feel our way through the rough, and then that inside path that I spoke about makes a sharp turn over and we can get onto that and follow it the rest of the way."

He went first now, to guard her from the occasional intrusive bushes or uncertain footing, while she back-seat drove him from across his shoulder to keep him going in the right direction.

"How is it they don't have the estate fenced in?" he asked. "Leave it open like this for anyone to trespass—"

"Too tight-fisted, I guess. They've owned it since the days of Peter Stuyvesant or somebody. You know these old families; they don't live much better than my sister does on Watt Street. Wouldn't spend a red cent for improvement or upkeep if it killed them! Maybe the old man would, if he could tell what he wanted."

After another few minutes they came unexpectedly out onto a little dirt lane, untended and barely visible beneath a patina of leaves and twigs. "Now the rest is all velvet from here on," she promised.

The path dawdled past a two-story building, a disused care-taker's lodge, the lower story of rough-edged boulders cemented together, the upper one of logs, with a sloping roof. The windows were all glassless, and the door opened flush with the ground. They stopped in front of it.

"Give me a match, Danny. I left a candle on the floor right inside the door when I was out here this afternoon."

"Got it?"

"Come in and close the door first."

Darkness smothered them like a feather bolster. Then a little-rayed star of matchlight twinkled between her fingers, widened into a candle flame, thrust out wavering tentacles, and sketched in the room for them in dusky-yellow line wash. It occupied the entire ground space of the building, and the candle gleam couldn't get into the corners.

"How do you get up?" He could see the black patch of an open trap over at one end of the ceiling.

"You don't. There used to be a ladder up through that, but somebody must have taken it away. This thing's older than the devil. I'm not sure that the flooring up there would hold anyone any more. You'll have to stay down here, Danny."

"How about the windows?"

"I took care of them as best I could. The ones facing toward the main house, I tacked green felt over them, from a bro-ken-down billiard table I found down in the cellar. The ones in back I had to leave the way they were. You're not in direct sight of the house from here anyway, but the thing to watch out for is someone prowling around in the open over that way and catching a chink of light from here. I've been busy here all week long, smuggling things out underneath the old man in the chair." She smiled a little. "Sometimes he sat six inches higher in it than he usually does, but luckily no one seemed to notice. I've been wheeling him out here for an hour or two every day and reading to him. But as long as he's out of their sight, they wouldn't give a damn where I took him. That's as much as they care about him."

She motioned to a double layer of blankets spread over a foundation of flour and potato sacking, flat on the floor. "That was the best I could do for you along those lines, Danny. I gave you the blanket from my own bed. I would have given you the mattress from it, too, but it was too bulky to lug over here without being seen."

He took her in his arms. They stood there together, silent. He found no words to say but she seemed content.

"I'd better be getting back now," she said.

"Can you get in or will you have to wake them?"

"I've got my own latchkey."

"Hadn't I better go part of the way back with you? That lane out there looked darned lonely just now."

"After all the trouble I just went to to get you safely in here without being seen? I guess not! I'll be all right, there's never anyone around out this way. Kill the candle, until you're ready to close the door again."

He went outside a few steps with her. "When will I see you again?"

"I wheel him out for air about eleven every morning. I'll slip over then."

"Don't take any more chances than you have to." He watched

her out of sight down the path until the gloom had blotted her out. Then he turned and went in and closed the door after him.

The candle relighted, he looked around the eerie, twilit place. He took off his coat and rolled it up for a pillow. He smiled grimly. "Home is the slayer," he parodied softly, "home from the sea."

18

His sensation, on waking up, was that of opening his eyes inside a grotto. All blue dimness. His bones ached from the plank floor and his neck felt as if it had a permanent kink. He unrolled his pillow and put his arms through its sleeves. Then he took down the green felt patches from the windows; she'd only used thumbtacks. Somebody might see them from the outside and think it strange.

There was no running water in the place and he had to go out and find some. It was a sort of arbored meadow out there, with plenty of big open saucers between the trees brimming with hot sun. A couple of white butterflies were chasing each other around, supplying the only bit of motion as far as the eye could see. The main house was well out of sight.

He finally saw what he'd been looking for. It wasn't much of a stream, not much thicker than a rope, but the water was clear and cold. He washed his face and drank some of it out of his cupped hands. Then he filled up an empty can with it for his coffee.

Ruth seemed to have thought of everything else. Over in the pantry of the main house they must have thought there were spooks about, the way things must have disappeared. Coffee, tinned milk, bacon, beans, even a container of sugar. There was a cobbled fireplace at one end of the room and he got a little twig-and-straw fire going in that, kept the embers alive long enough afterwards to heat his coffee over them. He was afraid to use large pieces of wood lest the smoke coming from the chimney betray him.

He was shaving by the touch system, over a tin can of slightly warm water, and with the detachable razor holder he'd brought out in his breast pocket from Tillary Street, when he caught an intermittent rustling sound, like something slithering over the ground in the stillness outside.

He jumped over to the door and crouched, peering out through the crack. It was only the rubber-tired wheels of an invalid chair Ruth was pushing up the path.

He stepped out and stared. In it sat an inert thing shaped in the likeness of the human form that might have been cleverly molded pink dough. The only things alive about it were its eyes. There was such a contrast between them and the body they were set in that for a moment Townsend received an illusory impression she was only wheeling two detached eyes, like car headlights, suspended at a height over the seat of the chair.

They gazed at one another in tense silence, the blueprint of a human being and the finished architect's design.

She said, with that slightly monotonous intonation used toward children, or the helpless, or the mute, "See? Look who's here, see? Here's your old friend back again? Are you glad to see him?"

It didn't seem those eyes could get any brighter than they already were, but they managed to.

Then she said, in a warmer, more lifelike tone: "How did it go, Danny?"

"Not a hitch, Ruth. You took care of everything."

"I could hardly close my eyes all night, I was so worried."

"Why?"

"To bring you this close. It seems such a scatterbrained chance to take, the more I think about it. You talked me into it down there last week, but— Why, this is the last place on earth you should be hanging around!"

He smiled quizzically and didn't answer. He was seeing her in her work outfit for the first time. It wasn't actually a uniform, rather the suggestion of one. She had on a dress of some crisp, yellow, starched stuff, and then over it two white strips crossing her bosom grenadier fashion, and a little apron of the same hanging from her waist. It was an improvement, he thought; it took away that untidy look: the tenement girl of Watt Street.

"Ah, he's waiting for you to say hello," she commiserated. She bent forward to look at her charge. "Don't disappoint him, Danny!" she urged plaintively. "Look how he's begging you to! I know what he wants." She laughed, bent forward, struck her own knees. "Don't you remember those swearing sessions you used to go into with him? You'd sort of trot out your whole vocabulary and use it on him, when there was no one around. Not because you were sore or had anything against him, but just in a kind of a lazy, good-natured way. But such language!" She chuckled reminiscently. "It was sort of like a code between the two of you. He actually enjoyed the abuse. I guess it was a kind of reverse way of showing you liked him. Go ahead, say hello to him. I'll clear out until it's over."

She took her hands off the guide bar of the chair, turned and strolled aimlessly aside. The eyes above the chair glinted.

It should have been very funny, but it wasn't. To Townsend it was poignant, almost tragic. He felt helpless, filled with a nameless sorrow.

He dragged down his collar with two fingers, swallowed hard, and began in a halting, labored voice that picked up fluency as it went along. It was a swell performance.

The old man's eyes were dancing with sheer joy when Ruth returned to the two of them, and Townsend was wiping off his forehead.

"It's wonderful, isn't it, how he likes the sound of swear words?" she murmured.

Afterwards, when they were sitting out there, one on each side of the chair, he remarked suddenly: "Why does he keep blinking like that?"

"The sun must be bothering his eyes." She shifted the chair around a little.

"The sun wasn't near his eyes," he said.

She leaned forward to look. "He's not doing it now, so it must have been that."

Townsend went on smoking for a moment or two, watching the motionless head in silence. "He's at it again," he said presently, in an undertone.

"Maybe *they're* going back on him too now, weakening from overuse." She touched apprehensive fingers to her mouth. "The poor soul, that's all he has left!"

He frowned as she sat back again in her original position. "He stops it whenever he catches you looking at him. He only seems to do it when I'm watching him."

"Maybe he's just trying to show you how happy he is to have you around again. What other way is there for him to show it?"

"He's *not* happy," Townsend insisted. "There's water forming in the corners of his eyes."

"That's right, he's tearing," she agreed. She took a handkerchief from the side pocket of the chair, touched it delicately to both sides of the graven image's nose bridge. "What does he want from you?"

"I don't know," he said helplessly.

"There must be something you've let him down about."

There must be, he thought, there must be, but who could tell him what it was? The only one of the three of them who knew couldn't speak.

She apologized for her continuing concern. Back at the main house, evidently, that would have been thought silly. "I don't like to see him cry. Now stop it, you here, Mr. Emil? It's been a long time since Danny was last with you; he can't be expected to repeat every last thing just as it was before. They get to be like children," she added in a pitying aside. "Did you used to give him things, like jelly beans or cough drops or something, out of your pockets?"

"I can't remember," he said with utter, forlorn truthfulness.

19

A LIGHT unexpected tapping at the door, well after dark, threw a short circuit into him. He'd been sitting there quietly smoking into the black fireplace when he heard it, without any warning sound of footfalls to precede it. He palmed the candle out with a flat, downward sweep of his hand, reared from the packing case he'd been sitting on, and stood astride it, tense and silent.

"Dan," the night seemed to breathe outside, "me." Or was that just a trick of the senses? He went over to the door, removed the chair barricade he'd uptilted against it, and put down the short iron crowbar he'd armed himself with.

"They went out about three quarters of an hour ago. I'd already put Mr. Emil to bed, and it was too good a chance to miss. I just had to slip over for a minute to see how you were getting along. Besides, I sneaked out some more supplies, in case you were running short."

"How is it I didn't hear you coming up?" he asked, helping her to carry the large carton across the threshold.

"Maybe because I'm wearing my sneakers. Dan, listen, I want to warn you. You'll have to be more careful about that candle; you'd better hood it or something, shut the light off on that side, toward the path out there. I could distinctly see a wink of yellow showing through as I rounded the turn of the path just now; there must be a crack underneath the window frame, and if it had been anyone else—"

He seemed to be thinking of something else. "Where'd they go, have you any idea?"

"I don't know, I didn't hear them say."

"Did they take the car?"

"Yes, but that doesn't mean anything, they'd have to, from out here, no matter where they were going. Why? What's on your mind?" She evidently didn't like the turn his questioning was taking.

"I want you to let me in over there, while they're out. I want you to show me the place, Ruthie."

Immediately she was aghast, filled with unreasoning terror on his account. "No, Danny, no! Be careful!"

"You said they went out, didn't you?"

"But there's no telling, they may come back any minute. Suppose they suddenly walk in on you? *Please*, Danny, don't."

He said with a quiet determination that wouldn't brook argument, "Take me over, Ruthie. I want to see it. If you won't, then I'll go over without you, on my own."

"You crazy fool," she mourned, following him falteringly out of the lodge and swinging the door after her. As they went down the path side by side in the darkness, she scolded querulously: "Instead of hanging around and hanging around, until something's finally *bound* to happen to you, you ought to be a thousand miles away from here and getting farther every minute while you still have the chance. You don't deserve *not* to have something happen, the way you keep going from bad to worse. I don't know why I bother my head about you anyway!"

"*I* don't know either," he agreed, tightening his grip on her arm, "but thank God you do."

It came sailing toward them at last, the outline of a house rearing against a luminous silver-clouded sky, indirect lighting furnished by a hidden moon. "So that's it," he breathed. She gave him a questioning little look of surprise. She didn't know that he was seeing it for the first time. The last roll of film had been underdeveloped; he hadn't been able to get any pictures from it.

He followed her up close to the front door. A peculiar quivery feeling cascaded down his spine. Now at last he was re-entering the very heart of the past, its innermost core.

She took out her key and opened, then prodded him impatiently through ahead of her, looking fearfully back across her shoulder. "Get in first, before I put the lights on. Get over to the side, where you can't be seen through the glass."

It lit up, and for the first time he was looking down the halls of murder. For the first time he, Frank Townsend, was seeing the place in which Dan Nearing had committed murder.

The house must have been as old as the hills, and pretty run-down. It had a brooding, depressing quality hanging over it, as though there hadn't been much laughter in it down the generations. Not so much active hate, as dourness and helpless frustration. There was a faint, teasing trace of gardenia left on the air. So vague that if you tried for it you couldn't get it; it assailed you only when you had forgotten it.

Ruth lit up a room on the left. "This was Mr. Harry's library and study—remember?" He saw her eyes rest on a painted iron plaque set into the paneling, then drop in embarrassment. He knew what she was thinking: that was the wall safe he was supposed to have burgled.

She killed the lights; they recrossed the hall laterally. "The living room, the same as when you were here." They went deeper into the house. "He's in here. Do you want to see him?" She put on the lights. The old man was lying in a tremendous bed, so big and wide he looked lost in it; he looked shrunken, like a limp rag doll. His eyes were closed, and his face looked more natural in sleep than it did awake. One makes allowances for a sleeping face; it is supposed to have that masklike look. The chair stood empty close up beside the bed.

"We leave him down here at nights now, in this little extra sitting room. Not like when you were here. The chair is too heavy for me to manage up and down the stairs twice a day."

"Do you put him to bed? What do you do about undressing him?"

"Well, I couldn't do that; it wouldn't be nice. I lift him in and out of the bed, yes, he doesn't weigh much. We leave him in this sort of sacklike flannel thing, it's really like a sleeping bag, and then I just put a robe and a comforter over him in the daytime, when he's up. Mr. Bill changes the foundation garment for him every two or three days—although I usually have to remind him. It's cruel when you're helpless, at the mercy of other people."

As her hand went out to the light switch, Townsend, turning away, received a momentary impression of one of the peacefully lidded eyes peering craftily open at them, but darkness followed too instantaneously for him to confirm it.

They went outside again, and he hesitated at the foot of the stairs. "Don't go up, Dan," she pleaded. "Your escape'll be cut off, if they happen to come back unexpectedly. There's nothing up there, just the bedrooms."

"What's that? I thought I heard somebody tiptoeing around up there."

"*You* know, that's Miss Adela, the—" She made a little circle with her finger close to her forehead. "She *never* sleeps. She's always creeping around and listening at her door, even when there's nothing to hear. I don't know why they've left her here in the house, instead of shipping her off to an institution. She hides when I bring her meals up, won't come out until after I've gone. Just the same, I never go in there backwards. Mr. Bill always carries the key to her room around on him, won't let anyone else have it. Like Mr. Harry used to in his day."

"Has she ever been examined? Has any outsider ever had a chance to look her over? How do they know she's actually—?"

"They say they had it done years ago. They say there's no use now any more."

"They say," he repeated laconically. "For all anybody knows, they may be getting away with murder. White murder."

"I used to try to make believe to myself that it was *her*. You know, to try to find an out for you in my mind. She was the only other person here in the house at the time, except the poor old man, of course. But—" She let her arms drop forlornly. "The key to her room was still on his body, and the door was still locked from the outside, when they came back."

They walked through an opening off side to the stairs and into a dining room. A bowl of wax fruit stood under a glass dome that might have been a hundred years old. Beyond, a double door stood closed.

She seemed anxious to go back, he noticed. "Come on, Danny, you've seen everything now."

He went on toward the double door.

"What do you want to go in there for?" she whispered. She tried to hold him back by the arm. "What good will it do?"

He already had them open, had the lights on. "What harm?" he parried inattentively.

She came reluctantly in after him. The glass was lined on the inside with strips of dark-blue roller shades, about one to every three pane widths. There was one that went horizontally across the ceiling too, like an awning, controlled by a drawstring from below. They were patched and mended in places. One of them had a little diamond-shaped rent that had not been repaired.

The room was floored in old-fashioned mosaic, gray with encrusted dust. It had two wicker wing chairs and a wicker settee. It had a long, low, tile-topped table running across one side of it, that had evidently held many of the potted plants and flowers in the old days. The whole enclosure was denuded of them now. A couple of dried-out, trailing, greenish wisps still lingered, swinging from pots hoisted on davits in the corners.

"Is this where he was sitting?"

Her face creased. "Dan, don't *talk* that way—!" She tried to cover her ears; he pulled her hands down. "As if you didn't know—!"

"Don't *look* at it! Come away from it!"

"Oh, I thought those were just rust streaks or something, from the nails in it.

"I don't know why they didn't throw it out long ago!" she flared. "I don't know why they've left it in here." She went on, more quietly, "But no one ever comes in here any more. It's the first time I've been near it myself since that day—"

"It's the first time I have, too," he murmured bitterly, as they turned away.

She reclosed the blue-shaded glass doors after them, with a

series of jiggling squeaks. They fell open twice, and she had to force them together.

He stood there, lost in thought. She came up close to him and buried her face against his chest. "Danny, Danny, why did you have to do it? You must've gone nuts when he said you'd been stealing from the safe. Why did you have that gun in your hands! If we could only undo that one afternoon. I would have loved you so. I still do, but I can't have you now."

He let her mourn it out. There was nothing he could say, no way to comfort her. She raised her head. "Come on, Danny, you'd better go now. You've been here long enough."

They repassed the stairs and went on down the hall. He fell behind a moment to light a cigarette. She reached the front door ahead of him, opened it narrowly to look out. Something went wrong. Suddenly a big golden sunrise seemed to beat in at her. The sound of brakes being thrown on punctuated the glare. A car door cracked open outside to coincide with her reclosing of the house door. Disjointed, breathless warnings flew from her like spray as she coursed back to him. "I *told* you—! The car—! They're back—!"

She pushed him before her around to the side of the stairs and in through the dark dining-room entrance. "The back! The back! Get out the kitchen door!" Then she took sudden root where she stood in sight at the far end of the hall, because a key was already pecking at the keyhole at its other end.

He just had time to take a floundering step forward before the front door had opened. The edge of a table caught him at the waist, blocked him. He moved around it, found a door, got it open, and started through into what he thought was the kitchen. Shelving bit into him in ridges from his forehead all the way down, and something that was glass or china pinged complainingly.

He managed to back out without knocking anything over. The table edge caught him again, this time across the small of the back. He got down on his haunches, and clung to it, one hand raised to its edge. He was hopelessly trapped there in the dark, in an utterly unknown room. He was afraid to move again, lest he collide with something and give himself away.

A raspy contralto voice was asking, somewhere outside: "Was that you peeping out at us just now?"

Ruth must have nodded, he didn't hear her answer.

"Then why the hell didn't you leave it open so I wouldn't have to go hunting for my key? What're you acting so spooky about?"

Ruth said, "I guess I must have fallen asleep, Miss Alma. And the lights of the car dazzled my eyes for a minute, you know how bleary you feel right after you wake up suddenly."

"We'll have to get you a pair of smoked glasses," the voice said ungraciously.

The whine of the car had shifted around to the garage, broken off short, and tin clanged shut on it.

The contralto voice was nearer the next time it sounded. It must have come down the hall to the back. A shadow flicked across the dimly lighted dining-room opening. "The picture was lousy. We settled for a couple of beers at the tavern." She was obviously unsteady, so the settlement must have been heavier than she was willing to admit. He heard her miss a step on the way up. He heard her mutter, "Pretzels and beer! Beer and pretzels! With God knows how many thousands of bucks in the kitty! I did better for myself when I was freelancing in Shanghai!" A bedroom door slammed above.

For tonight it was all right. Her perceptions were a little blurred. But would she remember in the morning the slight dissonance in Ruth's reception of her? Would she start wondering about it?

The front door closed and the latch went on. Someone else had come in. His mood was as sour as his predecessor's. "Back to the old homestead," Townsend heard him grunt. "Be sure you wake me in time to milk the cows in the morning."

Townsend heard a brief scuffle. He heard Ruth say sharply, "That'll be all of that!" There was a snigger and a heavy tread going up the stairs.

Townsend straightened up, came out around the table, and met her as she edged in on her way through to the kitchen. The start she gave showed she thought he'd gone already. "Danny! What's the matter with you? Why didn't you *go?* D'you know what could have happened to you if one of them had come back here for a drink of water or something? As a rule that's the first thing they do after they've been out drinking. Lucky they just didn't happen to tonight!"

"I couldn't find the way out, I got balled up in the dark."

"This way, what's the matter with you!" She urged him toward a screened opening, unseen until now. *"Please* go now, Danny. Haven't you taken enough chances for one night?"

As he stepped out into the darkness, she whispered after him reproachfully: "I can't for the life of me understand how you should come to get mixed up like that and not be able to find the way out."

He only answered that inwardly, after he was at a safe distance: "Because I was never in there before."

20

THERE WAS a certain tree down around the turn of the footpath which they had agreed upon as the safety zone beyond which he ought not to venture. They called it their meeting post. He used to go down and wait beside it for her to come along the path.

She'd come along a mottled tunnel of light and shade, one minute yellow disks of sunlight falling on her through the leaves, the next cool blue shade. He used to amuse himself by watching her slow progress down this long alley. Whatever the old man in the chair got first, she would get a moment later as she passed under the same place in turn; they never both got the same thing at once, sunlight or shade.

She'd see him from way up ahead, since he wasn't trying to hide, was just standing there openly, and she'd always go through the same little performance. First a guarded look backwards to make sure she wasn't being followed or seen from a distance; then his greeting, a pendulumlike swing of her hand, a little over her head, two or three times. She could make a passage of her hand, like that, seem as tenderly adoring as a kiss somehow exchanged across yards of open distance. And then finally, as he'd take a step or two forward each time, she'd always warn him back with a forbidding shake of her head, and scold him for it when she'd reached him.

"I've told you *not* to do that! Even this is too far out for you to come! One of these days when we least expect it, there's going to be someone drifting around over there; it always happens that way!"

But he had no time to worry about that now; he had something on his mind.

First he scrutinized the old man carefully. The eyes kept flickering up at him. "He's still doing it," he said to her. There was relief in his voice.

"He doesn't do it to a soul back at the house. I've been watching him closely, ever since you first called my attention to it."

"You didn't mention it to any of them, did you?"

"Of course not, what do you think!"

When they had reached the shack entrance, he said: "Did you get me those things I asked you for?"

"I went down to the village this morning. I've got them here in the side of the chair." She passed them to him singly. "Here's a pad of paper, and here's a couple of pencils. And here's the little pocket memorandum book. Is this the kind you wanted? I looked them over very carefully, and this has all those things printed on the first few pages. The capitals of the forty-eight states and stuff about the tides and the moon and birthstones and what to do for sunstroke and snakebite—"

"Well, I don't want any of *that* stuff, but I do want—" He leafed through it hastily. "Yes, it's here. Now I'm going to take him inside with me. Let me know when your time's up. You stay out here until then and keep your eye on the path."

She had a disappointed look, as though—well, if it were at all logical for an attractive, able-bodied young girl to be jealous of a man of seventy paralyzed from head to foot, it would have been that kind of look. "But what're you going to do? You haven't even told me yet."

"I'm going to try something, and if it works out, I'll tell you what it is afterward. If it doesn't, then that wasn't it anyway, so what's the good of worrying you with it?"

He wheeled the chair in after him. From then on there wasn't a sound from within the shack. How could there be? Whatever the means of communication he was trying to open up with this living tomb, it had to be a silent one.

She stepped inside the doorway about an hour and a half later, stood watching the two of them for a puzzled moment. Townsend had the old man's chair turned around so that the light from outside fell full on his face. He had the stenographer's pad that she had got him open on his knee, was rapidly streaking marks on it, eyes attentively on the old man's, furling the pages around one by one as his jumping pencil got to the bottom of them.

"What're you doing, trying to take down his *winks* in shorthand?" she exclaimed. "Does it *work*? Are you getting anything out of them that way?"

"I can't tell yet. I'm just notching them down as they come."

"But how can you do that? Isn't every wink just like every other wink?"

"That's what I'm hoping to find out. If it is, then I'm just wasting my time. But he keeps on sending 'em; he hasn't stopped once since he's been in here. There must be *some* coherent message in them, and that's what I'm trying for. I'll work on this tonight, when I'm alone—"

"Dan, you'll have to let me have him now. I gave you as much time as I could, but I'm way overdue for lunch, and I don't want to get them suspicious, they'll wonder what's been keeping me."

He got up, wheeled the chair out to the open for her. "Try to get back with him this afternoon if you can."

"But even if you do get some kind of language out of his blinking at you—what good will that do?"

"Maybe none at all," he said. "But if there's anything he can tell me, I've got to know it."

"Don't come any farther than this. They might be out looking for me. I'm thirty minutes late now. Wait a minute, this'll be good for an out." She nipped at the stem winder of her cheap little wrist watch, set the hands back. "My watch was half an hour slow." She stroked her lips fleetingly across his, grabbed the handle bar of the chair from him. "Hang on tight, Mr. Emil! I'm afraid you're going to have a rough ride back."

Townsend stood there by the tree, watching her down the leafy alley. Now the disks of sunlight and patches of shade didn't gently alternate down on her; they streaked in one continuous, blurred line like a striped tiger pelt, she was running so fast.

Suddenly the end of the alley showed blank and she was gone.

She returned that afternoon, although so long after her usual time that he'd given up hoping for her. He could tell at sight that she was frightened, something was worrying her. He went out to her.

"What's the matter? Did something happen?"

"I don't like the way she's acting. I'm afraid we're going to be in for it. She's caught on there's something up, I could swear to it!"

"Why, did she say anything?"

"She doesn't have to. I know her well enough by now. She wouldn't anyway. She's lived by her wits all her life herself. She knows all the signs. *She* doesn't give any warning. I wouldn't have dared come back here now, only I heard the shower going up in her room, and by the time she gets through putting on the last coat of shellac afterwards, it'll be another two hours. We'll have to do something, Danny; you better clear out of here before—"

"Well just what makes you think she's suspicious?"

"She was at her melon already by the time I got him to the table. I gave her the stall about my watch being slow, and she didn't say a word. Then when she got up, she moved around the table on her way out of the room. Before I knew what she was doing she'd stopped by his chair and picked up that damn book I've been packing back and forth with me, pretending to read aloud to him all these days. It was a trap, and I'd never tumbled to it the whole time. I'd selected a good long one, *War and Peace,* to make my spending so much time out of the house with him seem plausible. It has one of those old-fashioned ribbon markers, you know the kind, that you pass between the pages to keep your place. Well, she opened it and looked. Then she said, 'You're a slow reader, Ruth. A remarkably slow reader.' And she sort of fixed her eyes on me, and honestly, Dan, they were like daggers pinning me down. 'Or perhaps,' she said, 'you're reading backwards,' and then she went on out of the room. I only caught on what it was when I opened it and looked myself, afterwards. There was a little dab of lipstick on the page, so small you could hardly see it. Her kind. She must have done it days ago, and like a fool I've let the marker stay in the same place ever since."

"That's not so good," he said slowly.

"What're we going to do, Dan? I don't think we're going to

have very much more time. I'm scared about her and I think it's going to rain. Then I can't bring him out here."

"All right, I'll work fast, see if I can finish up what I'm doing this afternoon, at one more sitting."

He had barely touched pencil to pad, his eyes on the old man's face, when she came floundering in again, incoherent with sudden discovery. "Oh my God, Danny! Coming straight for here! I caught a flash of her through the trees! Give him to me! Give him to me, quick!" She almost overturned the chair, wrenching it out after her backwards. He started after her. "No, you haven't time to get out the door, she'd spot you through the trees, she's too close—"

He funneled up the litter of loose sheets of paper with a great double sweep of his arms, then opened his coat and buttoned it over them, holding them in place with both hands on the outside, as though he had a cramp in his middle. It was impossible to get up through that hole into the loft above, the ladder had been removed. He stepped in behind the door, which was folded back inward against the wall.

Ruth must have had just time enough to fling herself back on the campstool and split open the book that had pointed the way to suspicion, before the intruder came upon her.

Only a woman could have hit the exact right note of impromptu casualness. "Oh, here's Miss Alma, see?" she cooed for her patient's benefit. "Coming to find out what we're doing all the way over here."

There was a brief silence, then the familiar scratchy contralto sounded at Ruth's side. "Well, what *are* you doing, now that you mention it?"

"Oh, I found this place quite by accident one day, weeks ago," Ruth answered, then nervously elaborated. "D'you remember that fierce downpour we had? I'd strayed too far from the house to get back in time to avoid getting drenched, so I ran like anything to get in where the trees were good and thick—and here it was, just made to order. I've been coming back ever since." She ended rather lamely.

"It hasn't been raining ever since," the other voice mentioned dryly. "Or has it?"

He heard Ruth give a disarming little laugh, assuming a placid obtuseness that refused to take note of the veiled thrust. She had to, there was no other choice. "When it gets too hot, it comes in just as handy, I wheel him in there to get him out of the sun."

"There's plenty of shade around outside." The other voice was toneless. It waited a moment, then added: "What's the inside like?" It was an obvious challenge intended to test the girl's reaction. It worked.

He heard a dull thwack as the book suddenly toppled to the ground. The pitch of Ruth's voice was too strident at first, before she could iron it out. "Oh, there's nothing to see—"

The threshold creaked slightly, as with the pressure of a single step. Then nothing more. She was looking, but she already knew enough not to come in very far.

Ruth was still talking to her oblivious back, trying to anesthetize the discovery that was imminent. "I've been fixing myself up little snacks in there, with some things I brought out from the pantry." Another deprecating laugh that sounded hopeless. "I don't know why I get so hungry between meals! I must have a tapeworm."

"I've heard of that," the voice said, deadly level as ever. "That's when one person eats enough for two, isn't it?"

She was still standing there, her eyes taking in everything.

And you don't look that long at the interior of a neglected shack unless you're sure there's something to be seen.

A whiff of gardenia filtered through the seam of the reversed door. The back of it was flattening his nose, and he daren't try to evade the pressure. Couldn't have even if he had wanted to.

So close it was a wonder they couldn't hear one another's breathing. What was she standing there so long for? Wasn't she ever going to move? Perhaps she had already decided that it was better *not* to see anything. That seemed even more dangerous.

She spoke again. Poised daggers for syllables. "Quite homey."

She nudged something with the toe of her shoe; it gave out a tinny sound. "You seem to have gotten quite a kick out of playing house out here by yourself."

Ruth's voice was completely self-possessed enough. It was the answer itself that sounded absurd. "It's sort of fun to fix up an old place and make believe it's your own—"

"Like Marie Antoinette at Trianon." And then with an almost imperceptible change of key, "I always did wonder whom she used to meet there."

Neither of the two women said anything more.

Only her breathing told him she was still there. Suddenly a pinkish scallop had adhered to the door edge, within a hair's breadth of his vised-in face. Four of her five fingers had curled about it, as if on the point of drawing it out.

The nails were like scarlet obsidian daggers. There was a ring on one of the fingers, and it was so close to his eye that the moderate-sized diamond it contained was blurred to the size of a walnut.

He couldn't get his head any farther away from them, the angle of the door joining the frame narrowed too much to admit it. Even in the mere act of flexing her fingers to withdraw them, there was a very good chance of their striking the skin of his cheek.

But they didn't. They opened and missed touching him by sixteenths of an inch. If he'd needed a shave, they might have contacted the stubble on his face, that was how close they were.

She had seen something that drew her away. Yet he would have rather had her stay, when he understood what the magnet was.

"Shouldn't these things get rusty?"

There was a little *plink* as she tossed something down again.

His razor blade, left on a scrap of paper to dry. He cursed inwardly.

The threshold creaked in reverse passage. The awful propinquity was over. He could feel his stomach fill out with released breath, and something wet tracked down the side of his nose.

Her next remark sounded from the open again. "I tell Bill he should have this property fenced in. Left open the way it is, on all sides, anyone at all could hide out in it. I never feel safe, even in the daytime. At least, while that man's still at large."

"What man?" he heard Ruth ask guilelessly.

The answer was bursting with double-edged meaning. Accusation was implicit in it. "*You* know what man I mean. Dan Nearing. The man who murdered my husband."

Ruth didn't answer.

"Well, I'll be getting back now. I was just curious to see the attraction that keeps drawing you out here day after day. I've noticed more than once that the tracks of Father's chair led off in this direction—I suppose you'll be sticking around awhile longer, my dear." She managed to get a fiendish distortion into the epithet that suggested grimacing, manual strangulation.

Ruth played out her part with beautiful consistency to the end. She jumped up and the campstool legs clicked hastily together. "Oh no, wait for me, Miss Alma! You've got me so frightened now myself, I wouldn't stay here alone another minute, not on a bet!" The rustling hiss of the chair wheels went speeding down the path.

The last thing he heard was the contralto voice already a considerable distance away: "Your hands *are* clammy—for some reason or other." She must have found some excuse for touching one of them.

Townsend came out of his hiding place feeling like a bath towel after three people have used it. Unless she was a whole lot dumber than she sounded—and he didn't think she was—she'd caught on somebody had been hiding out in here lately, even if she didn't guess he'd been there at the same moment she was.

He released his compressed burden of papers, started to pry at one of the warped floorboards with the saw-toothed lid of a can for lever.

Need for food drew him back to the shack, after darkness had safely fallen. He'd been out of it all day, hidden among the trees, turned into a woodland thing now, without even a roof over his head. He wanted to side-step any possible surprise raid that her denunciation might bring on. He intended to sleep out. It was a clear, warm night, and there would be no harm in that. He could snag one of the blankets Ruth had provided for him and roll up in that; there wouldn't be such a vast difference between the bare ground and the lodge flooring after all. But first he had to get something into his stomach, even if it went down cold.

No Indian brave ever stalked a lone cabin in a clearing more craftily. He worked his way up toward it from the rear. He huddled motionless for a long time, screened by the trunk of a tree, listening. If there'd been anyone hiding in there, they couldn't have remained so silent for so long. Reassured at last, he slithered up close to the back wall, rounded the corner, and crept along the side toward the front, bent carefully low to make as little outline as possible, even in the gloom. Arrived at the outermost corner, he stopped again and listened. The dirt path before him was lifeless. The lodge itself was empty.

He moved again, covered the short remaining distance toward the doorway. The door was slanting inward now, whereas he'd left it closed. That worried him for a minute, but maybe the wind had done it.

He saw the white square adhering to the door, up near the top, on the inside. He could make out lines of writing on it, even in the dark. He took it down. It had been stuck in with a bent pin or piece of wire, and that flew out.

He closed the door first, then he struck a match, carefully shielded it from raying too far out under the front of his coat. He held the paper before it. The paper turned salmon, the lines on it sprang into legibility.

Dan—I've found out something terribly important. You will have to see it with your own eyes. Come over to the house at nine. I'll fix the door so you can get in. They won't be here, they're going into the city, so don't worry.

RUTH.

He studied it carefully, longer than seemed necessary to take in its simple meaning.

He'd only had one other piece of writing from her, the note she'd left for him that morning at Tillary Street. He looked to see if he still had this. He did, stuck away in his rear trouser pocket, with little clots of wool dust sticking to it. Funny that he should have kept it until now. Not so funny, maybe. Lucky. Darn convenient that he should have kept it until now.

He held them both with the same thumb, fanned out side by side. Then he struck a fresh match, poised it over them.

The match went out in his hands. He put the two pieces of paper back in his pocket. He had a few things to do before his rendezvous at nine.

21

THERE WAS a blurred moon up, and it spilled a platinum-gray wash over the house.

He came out from under the trees and stood looking across at it for a while, without moving. Not so much watching it— he knew there wouldn't be anything to watch for—as thinking things over. To go in there was final. He couldn't be wrong more than once. This was the once, right now, and there'd never be a twice.

This was the story's end, one way or another. This was the night. This was the time. This was the place.

His thoughts were a little like those of a man about to enter an execution chamber. He thought of the rag doll with the piquant face, Virginia. He thought of Dan Nearing's sweetheart, Ruth. He thought of the strange story that he'd lived, his own story. The first placid, uneventful twenty-five years. The three lost years; not fully visualized even yet, even with the aid of Ruth's eyes. Never to be entirely regained. The dismal, fugitive life that came of a blending of the two. And tonight—either an end or a beginning. The beginning of a fourth life. Four lives in thirty years. Whatever happened, he'd never be quite like other people again.

There it was, waiting for him over there, across the dim level of the lawn. Dark on all sides, not a light showing. Not a sign anyone was in it.

It was nine o'clock.

He started forward, closed in across the lawn, to keep his rendezvous. The short grass hissed under his feet, and a wavering black shadow like running water coursed after him, for he was going against the moon.

He went up the two low flagstone steps, a moment later was at the inscrutable doorway. His shadow, tacking, stood up against it like a cut-out litmus-paper man. Doorway to the past and to the future.

The knob felt cold and glibly elusive under his touch. *Here I go,* sparked in his mind. His belt buckle followed his stomach inward, closing the gap his tightly indrawn breath had left. He flexed his wrist and the door gave way before him. The latch had been fixed for him just as the note had said it would be.

He closed it after him. The darkness of the interior lay as thick and palpable upon him as a drift of black feathers. It all but tickled his nostrils. He reached over to the left, found the electric switch, pressed it. Nothing happened. The bulb in the fixture must have burned out. Or been removed.

The futile clicks went chasing one another down the dark of the hallway, magnified by the silence until they sounded like rumbling balls. It wouldn't have surprised him to hear pins go over at the other end.

He started forward, arm half bent before him in a vague swimming gesture, to guard against collision. An even deeper darkness, floating over the darkness that was already there, to one side of him, frizzed the hair on his neck for a minute, but it was only his own reflection flitting across an invisible mirror. It had stopped, with utter synchronization, as he did himself. He remembered, now, the night he'd been in here, having noticed one hanging at just about that place.

He went on again, dragging the shadow off the mirror after him. He stopped at the foot of the staircase, gave a short inter- rogative whistle. Two notes, one up, one down. You hear it on the streets a lot. Meaning: Hey, there! Where are you?

He repeated it, and the second time it got results. He heard a cautious tread coming out along the upper hall. It was very soft. There was stealth implicit in every lightest scuff of it. When it reached the boundary of the railing enclosing the stair well up there, directly over his head, it stopped, hung fire, as though the person were leaning over, silently questioning the gloom below.

"It's me, Ruth," he whispered huskily.

The answer came down blurred with excess of caution. "Shhh! I'm com' ri' dow'."

The tread started down the left-hand branch of the forked upper stairs and, as it reached the intersection midway down them, he could see an outline vaguely, like a ghost riding the dark above his head. He could make out the two white cross strips of Ruth's familiar uniform and the apron below, like something outlined in faintly luminous paint.

The apparition descended toward him, stopped about four steps above him. He saw the white of an arm reaching out to- ward him. A voiceless whisper went with it. "Give me your hand. I want you to follow me—"

"Wait a minute, I'll light a match—"

"No, don't! Give me your hand," she insisted. "I'll lead you."

She refused to shorten the distance between them. She

seemed stubbornly determined to force him to take the steps that would close the short gap between them. The white pad that was her hand stretched out demandingly toward him, across the gap. He clasped it with his own, felt the warm smoothness of her skin. Her second hand came out and joined the first, sidling about his wrist. It could not close entirely because of the bulk.

He started up and she began to draw him on, to make him come faster. The warning scent of gardenia touched his brain. The outstretched arms suddenly folded up at the elbows like treacherous levers, drew him in close and fast with unexpected, clinging strength. He lurched upward off balance. A taut rope stretched from bannister post to bannister post caught him just below the knees, and he went floundering helplessly down at nearly full length, face buried against other, softly impeding knees. A shattering shriek rent the air over his head. "He's down, Bill! Get him, quick!"

Something crushingly heavy flung itself down upon him from behind, pinning him there in floundering confusion, while he wrenched to try to get his hands free and bring them into use over arm and backwards.

All he succeeded in doing was to bring her entire, resisting body up short against him.

"Have you got him, Bill? Have you got him? Hurry up, he's killing my wrists!"

A male voice spoke for the first time, winded with effort, and so close behind his ear that he could feel its warmth. "Gimme his hands! Bring them together and bend them over this way—"

A knee at the back of his neck was holding his face ground into the concave joint where two steps were seamed together, pushing the soft part of his nose awry to one side. He kept trying to thresh free, but the dead weight resting on him crushed resistance.

She crossed her own arms, which were, while she was able to maintain her clinging grasp, simply a continuation of his, and thus brought his together at the wrists. "Here they are, here they are—quick!" Something that felt like a leather strap twined around them, first snugly close. Then its ends were twined spirally, cruelly, crushingly tight, so that the wrists pancaked over one another in tormented compression.

"There. Now just hold him where he is a minute. Put your foot on him so he'll stay down, until I can get up."

The crushing weight lifted from his back, was replaced by the sharper pressure of a woman's shoe, riding crosswise over the back of his neck like a tiny tapered boat mastering a swell.

The female voice, and only now, that it was neither whispering sibilantly nor screaming hectically, could he recognize Alma Diedrich's raspy contralto, said: "God! What he did to my poor hands! They're tingling as though they were frostbitten!"

The man, standing at full height over Townsend and still breathing heavily, said: "Got the bottle?"

"I stood it up there on the floor by the top step. I was afraid it would break."

"All right, bring it down. It'll make it a lot easier."

The foot left his neck, and a thick powerful hand replaced it, forked to hold him supine. He scissored his legs, but the man holding him avoided them by moving up two steps higher on the stairs.

"I can't breathe," Townsend gasped. "Let me get my face out—"

Bill Diedrich didn't answer, just kept the pressure even.

The woman came treading deftly down again, and there was a tiny murmur of liquid inside glass.

She said, "Can they tell afterwards when you've used this stuff on them?"

The man didn't answer that. "Are the shades all down? All right, we may as well do it right here on the stairs, it'll save a lot of trouble. Take this and give me a little light, so I can see what I'm doing."

The man sat down now, across Townsend's shoulders, holding his head as in a vise between sinewy thighs. A pocket light clicked into pallid being, found his face, dazzling him after the long darkness.

The liquid gurgled again, as though it had changed hands.

The man said, "Hold his head up off the step. He can't hurt you, I'm holding down his arms with my knee here."

His head suddenly bent upward, from the neck only, at an acute angle. She had him by the hair. The whites of his eyes showed against the torch beam.

Something small, like a stopper, went down on wood with a tap.

The liquid gurgled more rebelliously this time, as though it had been reversed within its container.

A freezing horror percolated through Townsend's veins. The horror that only comes of not knowing precisely what's going to be done to you. The terror of imagination.

A cloying reek swirled around his head. A soaked pad closed in over his mouth and nose from behind. He was only breathing sickening sweetness, not air any more. He tried to get his nose out of the way, from side to side, but the application just rode with it, backed up by a hand. He could still see over it, for a moment or two longer. A pair of eyes, reflected luminously against the torch glow, stared into his with pitiless, clinical interest. Then after a moment they started to blur.

He could still hear for a moment or two more after that, even after sight had dimmed.

"Watch his eyes and lemme know when he's had enough—"

Then hearing went, creeping away into the distance.

"There he goes. They're closing."

Feeling went last of all. He felt one of his eyelids prodded up, then allowed to droop down again, through no muscular reflex of his own. Then it was all jerked out from under him, like something on a rug: hearing and seeing and knowing and being.

The anesthetic wore off sometime during the next quarter hour or so and left a brief nauseous reaction that reminded him of the time he'd had his appendix out years before. Only this time, he knew, the operation was still to come.

He was in a sloped sitting position, shoulder blades but little higher than his kidneys, across what felt like the projecting seat of an overstuffed chair. For a moment he mistakenly thought his hands had been freed, the harsh bite of the bonds was no longer there. But when he tried to spread them, instantly constriction caught at them again, this time through the insulation of stiff leather. They'd been rebound over driving gauntlets, presumably to leave no telltale traces of chafing on his wrists. From that fact he deduced that at some future time it was to be made to appear that he had not been bound.

The shade or shades were drawn, but there was enough of a gap left at the bottom for a glimmering of moon wash to boil over and spill across the sill.

Something thick and braided was holding him fast to the chair; it felt like the sinewy multi-stranded sort of cording that is used to sash drapes and is almost impossible to break. One coil of it passed under his chin, directly across his throat. Too much pressure against it at that point would have garroted him.

For the first moment or two he thought he was alone in the room, although something that sounded like labored breathing had faintly caught his ear once or twice. But the flow of moonlight across the window sill was not static; as the moon climbed upwards over the house, the bar of reflection on the wall opposite to the crevice was foreshortened, began to be pulled down it to the bottom. It was at about elbow height from the floor when he first saw it. In a very few moments' time it had struck the top of a sofa immediately under it and begun to billow downward over the convex surface of that.

The first betraying turmoil of hair that it silvered, like a squashed-down halo, told him Ruth was in the room with him. She must be absolutely motionless, for the glimmering head made no move.

He spoke to her across the darkness long before the luminous visor had reached her eyes. "Ruth!" he whispered urgently. "Ruth!" She didn't answer. Why so silent? What had they done to her? He'd have to wait for that cauterizing bar to climb down to her eyes.

When it had, they were wide open, staring at him in helpless, limpid appeal. He knew that she must be gagged. He wondered why they hadn't silenced him as well. Perhaps because a woman is far more likely to scream out than a man. More likely, she had already been bound up in here when he had edged into the trap, and they had made sure she couldn't warn him.

People in peril don't make memorable remarks to one another. Language is apt to be anticlimactic at such times. He could think of nothing to say to her but: "Hello, Ruthie." Then he tried desperately to think of phrases that might comfort her. Nothing came to his mind, but he forced himself to speak to her several times, while the moonlight lingered on her eyes. Things like: "It'll work itself out all right. Something'll turn up." And once, in complete inanity, "My feet are asleep, how about yours?" Simply to keep her going, take her mind off their danger. He must keep her going a little while longer.

It was pathetic when her eyes went up into the darkness, as the bar worked its way lower down her face. It was like someone drowning in reverse. She writhed and tried to lower her head, to keep this window of visual communication open between them another half moment, another ten seconds. Finally she couldn't overtake it any more, her eyes went up into the smoldering gloom, and the gag across her lips slowly came into view.

A door opened somewhere upstairs, softly in the silence, and his skin prickled all over. "Steady, now, steady," he slurred reassuringly across at her.

A man's tread was coming down the stairs. It hit floor level, came on toward the closed door outside. The door opened, a switch snapped, and the room shot into unbearable, blinding brightness. When his eyes began to function again he was getting his first good look at Bill Diedrich, standing motionless in the open doorway.

He was squat and thick-set. He had that yeasty look that light-haired people get when they've hit dissipation beyond a certain point; his complexion was the color of unbaked dough. His hair was straw-colored, with a nasty tight little crinkle in it. He looked as if he might have been a nice guy—if he'd been somebody else. He had on a plum-colored bathrobe over blue rayon pajamas. Townsend knew he hadn't been either sleeping or bathing. The costume must be part of the act. He'd undressed for the murder, for reasons best known to himself.

He'd brought a revolver down with him, was holding it negligently, muzzle pointed to floor.

He grinned at Townsend.

Then he turned his head. "Alma," he called impatiently. "Are you ready? Hurry it up. I want to get this over with." He crossed the room and took a precautionary hitch at the shades, so that the gap below was effaced. Then he went back to the doorway again.

Another step came down the stairs. The woman's form joined his in the opening. The ubiquitous gardenia fragrance came back with her again. She was a little white in the face herself, with nervous tension, but there was no other sign of indecision. Townsend didn't waste much time looking her over, kept his eyes on the man.

Diedrich stabbed a hand impatiently at her coiffure, rumpled it. "Lookit your hair, like you just came out of a beauty parlor! Get a little realism into this, will you! What's the idea of the hat and coat?"

"I'm going out, you fool, to get the police! With the phone wires cut, what other way is there?"

"Yeah, but not looking like you just came out of a bandbox. We were in our beds when this guy tried to murder us. When you run out of a house for your life, to bring help, after you've just seen what you're supposed to have seen, you don't stop to put on a hat and coat!" He tried to control his fury.

"What d'you want me to do, drive down to the village naked?"

"Put on a robe over that nightgown, like I've got on me. And bring in that knife when you come back. There's something I want you to do before you go."

They were both so matter-of-fact about it. They might have

been discussing what clothes to wear to a show. Well, as a matter of fact, they were.

So that was what it was going to be. A murder masquerading as a legitimate case of self-defense. Well, they had the law on their side. He was a wanted killer. Not too many questions would be asked. And Ruth would go with him, to shut her up.

She came back with a long-bladed kitchen knife, attired now in the more appropriate dishabille he had indicated.

"What d'you want this for?" Townsend thought he could detect a note of heightened nervousness in her voice. She didn't mind his committing a murder, but she didn't want to have to see it happen in front of her eyes.

"This guy's supposed to mark me up, before I drop him. I can't just get away without showing anything. You do it for me."

"For the love of—!" she gasped.

"It's gotta be done! Come on, this is no time to be finicky. As long as you don't have to show any nicks, what do you care? Just don't dig in too deep, that's all."

He tensed his forearm, like someone about to have a blood count taken. "One across there. The back of it, not the inside. Easy, now."

They did it right there standing in the doorway. She closed in so that her back was to Townsend. He couldn't see the act itself, but he could see the man's face across her shoulder, looking absorbedly down. It twitched slightly.

"Don't close your eyes like that," he instructed coldly. "You're liable to bungle it. Now try one on the chest."

The rearward point of her elbow moved slightly.

"Whew!" He sucked in breath with the sting.

"Now a thin one across the forehead. Just with the point of it. Careful now, I don't want to have to take stitches."

That time Townsend could see the blade move. It traced an invisible line, that only reddened moments afterward. She stood back. "Hurry up, we haven't got all night."

He was blowing along the upraised side of his arm, to try to cool it. "All right, get the car out."

It was their cold-blooded matter-of-factness that lent such grisly horror to the situation. If they'd whispered, if they'd glared, if they'd leered. But they were talking it over as if she were going on an errand to the grocery store and he was promising to repair some household gadget for her while she was gone. Townsend in his time had heard more dramatic emphasis displayed about the destruction of a mouse.

They turned and went out into the hall together, stopped just short of the front door. They remained faintly audible out there for a moment or two longer, while he gave her last-minute instructions, impressed upon her what had already been arranged between them.

"It's nine-twenty now. It'll take you thirty minutes in and back, even doing sixty. *Don't bring them back under that,* whatever you do! Can I rely on you? I'm going to need a good half-hour, at least, to get rid of the portiere cords and fix them the way they should look. If you find that you've gotten to the police too fast, throw a faint or something from fright, tack on another five minutes that way. But make sure you do it *before* you tell them what's happened. Once you've told them you won't be able to control their speed getting back here. It'll be out of your hands, and those state highway cars shoot fast. Remember, *thirty minutes.* Here's the garage key."

The front door opened. Townsend heard her parting remark. "Bill, will we ever be able to sleep again?"

And he heard the sound of a kiss, and the answer that went

with it. "I'll stay awake nights from now on for the two of us. You can buy a lot of sleep with a dollar sign. This is on me."

So there was love in it. Love of a sort. It hadn't been only for money that they had wanted Harry Diedrich out of the way.

The door closed. He didn't come right in again; he must have stood there waiting by it, to see that she got off in good order. Townsend could hear the hollow sound the car engine made starting up inside the garage walls. Then it thinned as it came out into the open, switched back and forth a little, finally opened up into an even hum and faded out down the cut off toward the highroad.

She had gone to get help—for something that hadn't happened yet. The murderer and the murdered-to-be were left alone together.

He came back along the hall, but his destination was still not this room, this execution chamber. He stopped in it a moment in passage to pick up the knife, went out with it again and on up the stairs.

He was very quiet about the whole thing. Little revealing sounds were all that came down. But then murder doesn't make much noise. First a key wrangled in a keyhole, somewhere up above. Either he was slightly nervous himself, or the aperture was balky from infrequent use.

Adela, the girl they said was insane. Kept locked in her room for years. A dollar sign, he'd said just now to Alma at the door. This Addie must be a beneficiary in the estate, insane or not. And this was her own brother, standing at the door, key in one hand, knife—probably—crouched behind his back.

The key had found its right depth and angle at last. Townsend heard the grunt the door gave in breaking away from its frame. Then Diedrich's voice, in casual, treacherous salutation from the threshold: "Still awake, Addie? I thought you'd be in bed long ago. Cook wants to know what you'd like for dessert tomor—" The door closed, cutting the rest of it off short.

There was a moment of utter stillness. About as long as it takes a person to cross a room. Townsend strained against the chair that held him, his mouth looped in a grimace of excruciation. He could feel Ruth's distended eyes burning into his face from the sofa opposite. He didn't have the heart to meet them; he ignored the mute appeal. There was something obsccne about having to sit and look at one another while such a thing was happening.

Suddenly a scream of animal-like unreason kited up, a sound that belonged in a slaughter yard. It stopped again as curtly as it had begun. Then there was a gurgling, slavering moan of dissolution. Then nothing.

He stayed in there awhile. Then the upper door reopened. Townsend heard a chair or bench in the upper hall go over. Not the clatter of an accidental collision. The sound had a careful, deliberate quiet. More stage setting, Townsend thought. The chair would look as though it had been overturned in the course of a hand-to-hand struggle.

His tread came on down, and he showed up in the doorway again. It was a terrible moment for Townsend. He was seeing what a man's face looks like right after he's committed murder. It was parchment yellow with lack of blood, as though the knife had drained *his* off as well as—someone else's. It was satiny with sweat, and he ran the tip of his tongue along his mouth to get some of it off his upper lip. He looked back, once, before he looked in at them. In the look back, though there was nothing alive back there now, was the racial heritage of fear and awe, no matter how fleeting, that always accompanies violent death.

He still had the knife in his grasp, three quarters of the blade hidden inside a red patent-leather sheath that frayed and unraveled off it as he stood there, letting the steel peer luminously through again in oily patches.

He was the killer still steaming from the kill. He was murder, on two legs and in the flesh.

Not a word had passed Townsend's lips until now, in all the time since the Diedrichs had first descended to the room. He had known that it would be hopeless, to plead or threaten or try to reason. But now a raging resentment simmered up in him, boiled over. He began to swear, in a hissing, monotonous litany. All his horror at the man who stood there was translated into inadequate language.

Diedrich smiled as he closed the door behind him. "That's what I call real big talk," he murmured with almost detached admiration, as though he were listening to a phonograph record. "It's a shame to have to deprive the world of such a vocabulary. Look out, you repeated yourself just then—" He came close, and for a minute Townsend thought, this is it. But he only touched Townsend lightly about the face a few times with the flat of the blade, like someone trying to make lumps disappear by pressing them with cold steel. He was daubing Townsend with telltale traces of a crime that wasn't his.

Then he wiped the handle carefully with a bit of gauze and laid the implement aside for the time being. It lay there waiting for Townsend's hand to close around it—after death.

He picked up the gun. He shot the clip back to make sure it was fully loaded, closed it again. He moved over into a straight line with the man on the chair, then slowly paced backwards six steps, like someone practicing for a duel. He was holding the gun sighted at Townsend, without a tremor of the hand, like someone taking aim at one of those two-dimensional ducks in a shooting gallery.

The little round black bore, centering at him, seemed to expand, to widen, to acquire an active drawing power of its own, as if it were trying to suck him in bodily, like a vacuum nozzle. He could almost feel himself leaning hypnotically toward it, as far as his bonds would permit.

"You better shut your eyes," Diedrich let him know grimly. "That'll make this easier on you."

A pulse in Townsend's cheek, up near the ear, started to tick. He didn't speak. He smiled thinly, way over at one side of his mouth. He forced the smile to stay on his face.

There's something about such a smile that troubles the beholder, that makes him wonder: What's he got to smile about at such a time? What's he got on me that I don't know about? The challenge worked.

Diedrich said, "What's funny?"

"You never heard about an angle of fire, did you?" Townsend had to moisten his lips to make them articulate. "You're firing *down* at me. I'm in a chair and you're on your feet. That's going to look great for self-defense. D'you think they won't notice that? Don't kid yourself." And the smile stayed waveringly on. It had a hard time, but it stayed on.

The way the gun went abruptly vertical, muzzle to floor, showed he'd made his point.

A minute gained? Forty-five seconds gained? Time was the enemy now.

Diedrich dipped one knee under him, tried to correct the discrepancy that way. It was no good, the course of the bullet would now be slightly upward. And the midway position, which would have been the right one, was too awkward. It was impossible to support steadily for any length of time. It required a slight buckling of the knees, a half crouch; he couldn't even be sure of his shot taking effect from such an unsteady stance.

The method he hit upon at last was almost ludicrous. But there was no humor in it to either of the men. Diedrich slung out a vacant chair and placed it in a straight line to the one in which his prisoner was bound. He sat back in it and raised the gun once more.

He didn't fire it. He was unsure now. The subtle objection Townsend had managed to insert into his mind must have kept on unfolding postscripts. There were other things to be considered in addition to the bullet's trajectory line. There was the position of the bodies afterwards. If the bullet entered in a certain way, then they must be found lying in a certain way.

He couldn't take any chances. Townsend had counted on that. Diedrich took what he imagined was the safest and quickest way out. He rose, strode impatiently across the room, and threw open the desk. He pocketed the gun momentarily, took out a scrap of paper and a pencil. Then he pointed—to the girl, to Townsend, to the floor. He was arranging them ahead of time, measuring the arcs of their body falls from the positions in which he wanted it thought they had met their deaths. Townsend could glimpse his marking hasty broken lines on the paper. He worked quickly, like a stage director setting a stage for a crime supposed to be impromptu, a crime committed in the heat of justifiable self-defense.

Once he went so far as to murmur raptly, with a stab of the pencil toward Ruth, "You over here."

It may not have been intentional cruelty. But a sadistic demon out of Dante's hell could not have improved upon it. The girl was almost cataleptic, half expiring. A curtain of beads was forming at the roots of Townsend's hair.

Finally, his blueprint completed, Diedrich tacked it to the outside of the sloping desk slab, for ready reference. He consulted his wrist watch briefly, as if to check on his accomplice's time schedule.

He gave a last comprehensive look around, to make sure everything was in order. No details of the general scenic effect could be overlooked. A chair that would have presumably impeded him in fighting for his life he hooked with his foot and allowed to crack over on its back, then painstakingly stepped over it in order not to disturb its prone position.

He rubbed his hands together a couple of times, to get their circulation up, like a surgeon about to perform a delicate operation.

Then he was ready for it at last.

He went over to Ruth, bent across her, and fumbled at the back of the sofa, where one of the portiere cords had been passed through the slit between back and seat to hold her on the seat.

Her eyes, peering out under his raised arm, gave a concentric swirl in their sockets, her head looped over. She had fainted away.

He seemed not to notice, or if he had, not to care. He freed her after a moment, picked her up bodily in both arms, and staggered out into the middle of the room with her. Her hands and ankles, which had been separately bound, he allowed to remain so for the moment. He set her down on the floor, with a gentleness that was hideous.

Her weight must have been greater than he had expected. A fit of coughing interrupted him before he could draw his arms out from beneath her. He swayed there over her, racked, for a minute. Even went down on one knee to retain his balance.

He stopped at last, got his breath back momentarily. Then Townsend began to cough.

There was something the matter with the air in here. Outlines, in places, weren't rigidly straight any more, were quivering, as if seen through sweltering heat or a dislocating refraction of some kind. The linings of his eyelids began to smart intolerably, protective water formed, and he could only see Diedrich liquidly, as in a trick mirror, one minute tall and skinny, the next squat and bloated.

He heard him go over to the door, still coughing, and stand there a moment, as if listening or questioning something. Woodwork buckled somewhere outside, as if subjected to some intolerable pressure. Diedrich reached out sharply at the sound, opened the door to look out.

What followed was as though a giant eraser had been stroked across his figure. He all but disappeared, faded into gray halftones. There was an added horror to the phenomenon because of its utter soundlessness. A great gust of dirty, flannel-thick smoke mushroomed in. It must have been accumulating out there in the enclosed hall for untold minutes, to acquire the density it already had. Instantly it had diffused itself everywhere, yet scarcely thinning at all as it did so. The room was gone, a sort of swirling twilight filled it, with only a soft-focused glimmer left where the light had been.

Townsend, through almost useless eyes, could glimpse a gray ghost form weaving its way back from the door, one purpose still uppermost in its mind even now, retching up its insides as it went.

Diedrich's foot must have struck the girl's submerged form.

He went down flounderingly, in a sudden full-length fall. The gun he had been holding ricocheted loosely almost at Townsend's own feet. He could see it lying there, outlined like a black T square through the thickening, stratified haze that was still thinnest down there by the floor. Then a hand came out, also along the floor, blindly groping for it, twitching spasmodically with the paroxysm of coughing still sounding somewhere out of sight behind the curling masses of gray-brown ostrich plumes.

Townsend tried hectically to reach it with his own foot and push it still farther beyond reach. He couldn't. Three times the tip of his shoe swiveled past in an empty arc, just missing it by inches. Then the crawling, buglike white fingers found it, closed hungrily, drew it back into the pall.

There was a fitful wink of orange light down close to the floor, and the room thudded with a blanketed detonation that seemed to send an outward swirl through the smoke curtain, dying out again lazily before it had traveled very far.

There was a moment of grisly expectancy. Then a face suddenly thrust out at Townsend at half level, as though the body under it were traveling along on bended knees, unable to lift itself erect any more.

A hand pointed waveringly toward him, its index finger black and thicker than the rest and holed at the tip. It swayed from side to side, missing him by whole feet in either direction. The light sparked again, what felt like hot sand stung his cheek and something thudded into the thick chair back alongside his face.

But he was hardly aware of all that any more. He didn't need bullets to rush him off, he was going fast enough. Every breath was more agony than the one before. They went down red hot, halfway to the bottom, then backfired and came up again, ripping the lining from his windpipe. His eyes had gone long ago, sizzling coals extinguished in their own fluid.

There was an inert, sodden clump from the floor right before him, and somebody's head landed on his knee, then sidled off it again, hit his foot and stayed there.

His own head was straining apart, getting ready to fly to pieces.

The last thing he heard was the far-off, useless tinkle of breaking glass.

22

THE OXYGEN going down his throat felt good. He was angry when it stopped. They took the tent off him. He was lying on his back out in the open some place, with an arrested blizzard of stars over him. There were talcum-white shafts of light criss-crossing along the grass here and there, and against them a motionless frieze of black legs stood outlined around him in a half circle.

One pair telescoped into a face that came down close to his. The near-by shine of one of the reflectors showed it to him.

He took a good long look at this face, and it took a good long look back at him. He knew it intimately by now, although it had never been this close to him before. Inscrutable, wooden-Indian face that never smiled. It had stopped and stared at him in the crowd. It had glowered balefully through a dusty subway-car window. It had been reflected through a drugstore window. It had started to turn and look along a day-coach aisle. It had even topped a pair of shoes that had followed him in a dream, without becoming visible itself. And here it was, as close as it could get now. It had caught up with him at last. It had him flat on his back on the ground. It had him pinned to the mat.

He spoke finally, with languid unconcern, "You're Ames, aren't you?"

"That's me," the face said challengingly. "And you're Dan Nearing, aren't you?"

"Like hell I am," he said. "I'm Frank Townsend."

They helped him up on his elbow first, and then to a sitting position. He found the oxygen had left him a little lightheaded. "Don't you ever change that hat?" he heard himself say to Ames.

On his feet again, he looked around. The Diedrich house was in the background, with interlocking circles like big white poker chips backed up against it by the reflector lights. An occasional whiff of pungent smoke drifted over from it on the breeze. There were people and apparatus standing around on the lawn. Life-giving apparatus and smoke-fighting apparatus. Cars galore, all run off the driveway and parked on the sod at various angles. There was an ominous-looking chassis with its back standing open. A small crowd around were watching something on a slab being pushed into it. Something covered up, with two peaks at one end that suggested uptilted shoes. A helmeted head appeared at one of the upper windows and threw something out on the ground below. The place was alive with activity.

They started to walk him, Ames on one side of him, a deputy of some kind on the other, giving him a hand with his footwork.

Townsend asked the question that he'd been thinking since his awakening. "What happened to the girl?" he said. He tried hard to keep his voice calm.

Ames gave his expressionless face a slight shake.

"He got her, didn't he? I heard the shot through the smoke."

Ames gave his face a dip this time.

Townsend savagely mouthed a short paternoster of damnation.

The face beside him said with characteristic taciturnity, "Save your breath. He's been fumigated, the way rats should be."

Townsend said, "She was a great kid. Without her—" His voice trailed off, and the three men said nothing more.

A group just ahead shifted aside to admit them as they came up. He could see another of those flat, covered-up things on the ground at their feet. The same chassis that had swallowed the first slab was backing up to pick up this one.

"Who's this—Ruth?" he faltered.

"No, we've got her down in the village already. This is the guy that saved your life."

"I don't get it. Who's that?"

Ames squatted down, tipped back the edge of the tarpaulin. "The guy that gave up his, for yours."

"The old man!" Townsend said contritely. "I forgot him for a minute! So he went too."

The rigid straitjacket of his disability had been obliterated by death. He looked like any other man in death. They'd closed the eyes, and the face looked placid, satisfied, yes almost triumphant.

Townsend looked down in silence. What was there to say?

"Did you know he'd retained a slight use of one hand, the right?" Ames said.

"Yes, I caught on to that. But only by accident, a couple of days ago, when she had him over at the shack with me. It wasn't much, he didn't have the full use of it by any means. He could turn back a couple of the fingers a little, and pivot slightly from the elbow, that was all."

"That was enough. Enough for him to get hold of a weapon."

"A weapon?" Townsend turned and looked at the detective.

"That's what it amounted to. The only kind of weapon *he* could handle. An ordinary, everyday, sulphur-tipped kitchen match. What d'you suppose all that smoke was, spontaneous combustion? There must have been a box of them within reach somewhere, on the edge of the range maybe, like in most kitchens. I guess he was wheeled in there at times and his chair accidentally left standing close to it. And each time he stole one or two of those matches. God knows what he thought he'd do with them."

Townsend said, "He had good ideas."

Ames shrugged and said, "He clawed a little rent in the mattress under him. It must have taken him a hell of a time. We found it stuffed with charred matchsticks when we carried it out into the open just now. It tells the story. He faced that death, not the easiest kind there is, to try to attract attention from the highway in time to save you. It wasn't much of a chance but it was the only one he had, and he was willing to take it."

"He did save me," Townsend said. "Even my own message would have gotten you here too late. Diedrich would have still had time to put a shot into me. It was the smoke, and not you fellows, that dropped him. As a matter of fact, he did hold out long enough to snap one at me, but he was too far gone by that time to aim straight. I think it went into the back of the chair."

"Was it you sent in that tip that if we wanted the killer of Harry Diedrich to close in here no later than quarter to ten tonight?"

"That was me," Townsend said dryly. "And if you've got any doubts, I asked to speak to you yourself, and you tripped over something getting to the phone. I heard it over the open wire. The foot of a chair or a desk, something like that."

"It was you," Ames conceded.

"I couldn't time it any closer than I did. If I'd gotten you here too soon, they would have pulled their punches, it would have been your hands I'd have been walking into, not theirs. They would have been just innocent third parties to the arrest of a wanted murderer in their house. If I timed it too late—bingo, you saw what nearly happened. It was a gamble, and I took it, and I lost. Only he called off my bet and gave it to me back."

"How'd you know they'd play into your hands, at just such and such a time tonight?"

"I got a decoy note from them, supposed to come from the girl. They'd caught on a few days ago I was hiding out around here. They didn't want me turned in alive—because they knew damn well I hadn't killed Harry Diedrich; they had. So they tied up the girl and then laid a trap for me. I caught right onto it, and I walked right into it of my own accord—with just the slight variation of tipping you people off about coming out here."

"Well, you sure played hob with the dame's timing," Ames admitted. "We were already on our way out here when she started in to get us. We met her a little below the Struthers house. For a person in search of help, she didn't seem too happy about meeting us. She went into her spiel anyway and she took a hell of a time telling us. She was so damn explicit, that was the trouble. Too damn explicit. We were going to find you both dead. She was sure of it. He'd had to, in self-defense. She even gave us the sound track on it. 'Are you all right, Bill?' 'I've killed them, Alma. Look, I've killed them both. They're both dead here on the floor. You better go out and get the police.'"

Townsend said, "I saw them planning it."

"The only trouble was, there was a slight discrepancy when we got here. She seemed to have gotten the cart before the horse." He came pretty close to smiling, which wasn't close. "Some people from a passing car had broken the windows and gotten you out by the time we got here. You were certainly not dead, even if the girl was. The give away was that you were both still trussed up hand and foot. They'd had to carry you out, chair and all, to save time. Self-defense can be stretched out pretty far at times. But tying two people up first and *then* shooting them to protect yourself is stretching it too far. And then, when we'd gotten the smoke out and looked around, a couple of other little things turned up. F'rinstance, this. Above all, this."

He took out the chart of fire angles and death positions Diedrich had tacked onto the desk front. "Guys that shoot in self-defense don't usually have time to draw pictures of it ahead of time."

Townsend said: "I suppose you still think I killed Harry Diedrich?"

"As a matter of fact, I don't, after what happened out here tonight. But," the detective let him know, "what I personally think or don't think has got nothing to do with it. There are charges outstanding against you, there's a warrant out for you, and if you didn't—*have you any proof you didn't?* That's what you're gonna need. I'm just the arresting officer in the case."

"Yes. I've got proof. Solid. Twofold. I've got an eyewitness account."

"An eyewitness! You were alone in the house with him—"

"Oh, no I wasn't! Aren't you forgetting—?" He nodded down toward the still form at their feet.

"Him?" The detective gave a start. "Now wait a minute—"

"His eyes were all right, weren't they? His chair was in that side sitting room the whole time that afternoon, wasn't it? He couldn't see in a straight line into the sun parlor, because, for one thing, the doors were closed. But he could hear everything. And he could see whoever went in there and came out, couldn't he?"

"Suppose he could—and did? He's dead now. And even if he weren't, he couldn't speak a word, his tongue was paralyzed along with the rest of him. How'd you get it out of him?"

"Go back to that shack where Ruth hid me out. Count back six floor boards from the door sill. Pull the sixth one up, it's loosened. In the trough under it you'll find a pad and a wad of loose scratch paper. That's his testimony, taken down by me at first hand."

"How?" said the detective skeptically. "By mental telepathy?"

"Through the eyes. In ordinary Morse Code, the way they tap out messages in every telegraph office in the country. A short blink was a dot, a long blink was a dash."

Ames said, "Well I'll be—! Why the hell didn't he try a little of that on me when I was out here working on the thing at the time?"

"You mean why the hell didn't you keep watching him long enough to figure it out for yourself. He practically broke his heart winking at you every time you came near him, he says so himself in his account, and you wouldn't stand still in one place long enough to dope it out. You probably just took it for part of his sickness."

"Yeah," Ames admitted, lowering his head thoughtfully, "something like that. And what's the second proof you said you've got?"

"I'll show you that. I'll let you see it for yourself. I'll show you that around midday tomorrow, weather permitting."

Two men came forward to pick up the inanimate form lying

there on the ground under the tarpaulin, put it in the back of the death wagon.

"Wait a minute," Townsend intervened, "let me say good-by to him first." He motioned to them. "We had a special way of talking together. It isn't usually heard at a time like this, it might shock you, but I want to sign off in the way he'd want."

Ames hitched his head and they wandered off a short distance, stood there looking over at him.

The man that had been Dan Nearing gazed down at the still face on the ground before him. Ames could hear his voice in a steady murmur. Only the last sentence was loud enough for words to be distinguished. "This is your friend Danny, saying thanks—and so long."

23

THE WEATHER permitted. It was bright and hot and still.

The place, drowsing in the sun, already had a deceptively somnolent air about it, as though all that had happened there had long been forgotten.

A cop posted at the door to keep away curiosity mongers was the only incongruous note. He rose from a rocker he'd dragged outside and settled himself again as the official car came into sight.

Townsend walked in first, Ames beside him, the others behind them.

They opened the doors of the sun porch, went in. It was full of dust motes dancing in the air.

Townsend said, "This is where Harry Diedrich was killed. I'll show you just how it was done, by Bill and Alma Diedrich, his brother and his wife, while they were miles from the house."

Ames folded his arms, tapped his fingers on his biceps, with an air of saying, "Go ahead, that's what I'm here for."

"It's just the way it was that day. Wicker settee, low tiled-top stand opposite it they used to stand plants on when this was used as a conservatory. I'd like to have something to mark the place of Harry Diedrich on this settee. It isn't really necessary, but it might help to have the whole picture."

"All right, one of the fellows here will—" Ames started to say.

"I think it better be something inanimate, unless you want to be minus a member of your force."

One of them brought in a medium-sized, glass-domed table lamp, stood it upright against the back of the settee. The greater part of the dome topped this, showed above it.

"That'll be about the right height," Townsend said.

"He came in here every day immediately after lunch and napped for about an hour. All right, that's him there. He's in here for his nap now, legs comfortably spread out along the settee, head showing above it in that corner. He slept with those dark-blue shades all drawn full length, to keep the light out of his eyes."

"D'you want 'em down?" Ames grunted.

Townsend smiled a little. "We want the whole picture."

One of the men got busy.

Townsend said, "I want you to keep your eyes on this tile-topped stand as the place darkens up."

It went down the chromatic scale, as shade after shade was drawn. Brilliant yellow white to yellow green, to greenish blue, to indigo. On the table, with every eye drawn to it, a diamond-shaped scar of livid light had leaped to life, cast by a matching rent in the shade above.

It wasn't the only one of its kind. The shades were frayed and threadbare in places, they'd been up a long time. All over the inward gloom they cast, on floor and table and wicker furniture, was a vague pattern of streaks and dabs and curlicues of reflected faults, like a sort of arrested rain of light. But the diamond-shaped scar was the most distinct, the largest. It was the only one of that particular clean-cut shape. So clean cut it might almost have been scissored out.

Townsend said, "He's in here napping and the shades are down now. He's in a deeper sleep than usual that day. The old man figured he'd been doped, just enough to make him sleep sound.

"I think I must have gotten some myself. I dozed off across the hall there, in the little side room where I usually wheeled the old man.

"Ruth and the cook were finishing up the lunch dishes, fast and noisy, in the kitchen at the back. Both of them had a half day off. They had planned to catch the two o'clock bus into the village. And the murderers knew it. So they weren't taking any chances in leaving first; they were making things look more plausible. Harry was a grouch and tyrant; none of the help would have dared come near this place to disturb him once he'd closed himself in for his afternoon nap. And naturally his brother and his wife knew that, too.

"So they came down the stairs, ready to leave. She got the car out and brought it around to the door, and he—here's what he did."

He reached toward one of the motionless figures standing around him. "Give me the shotgun. Has it been loaded?"

"I reloaded it before we came out."

Townsend took it over to the door with him, turned the knob, opened and closed the door without moving from it, then came forward again shotgun in hand.

"By that, I mean he stepped quickly aside to the storage closet behind the stairs, when he followed her down, and got this out. It was always kept there. It was all readied and primed from the night before, he'd seen to that. He stepped quickly in here with it. Only one pair of eyes saw him, and he didn't give a hang about them, because they were set in a head that couldn't talk.

"He came in here with the gun, and he cocked it open so that the charge was exposed, and he laid it down across the stand like this."

He lowered it carefully, so that its foreshortened muzzle pointed straight at the lamp propped in the corner of the settee.

"There were marks on this table to guide him. Not the kind you might have found when you looked around later. But marks just the same. These crevices between the tiles, to act as parallels of latitude and longitude. To make them workable all he had to do was adjust the feet of the stand itself on the floor, shift it slightly forward or back, so that this diamond of light would be sure to fall on and follow the lengthwise seam between the tiles for a considerable distance over, before it finally curved off it. And the crosswise seams, they were like the hands of a clock. He'd carefully timed it ahead of time, found out just how long it would take the light mote to travel along from one to the next. What it amounted to, I don't know. Say it was ten minutes. One and a half tile widths then would give him a quarter of an hour. Much the same basic principle as a sundial.

"So all right. He didn't put the gun immediately under the light mote. That wouldn't have given him any headway. He set what amounted to a time bomb. He set the gun down a certain distance to the right, still far off side from the combustive diamond, but in a straight line along which it was bound to pass in a given number of minutes. Say I foreshorten it for our purposes, make it a half square."

He did so. Stepped around and away from it, and motioned his gallery likewise. "All this didn't take him as long as it has taken me to tell it. He stepped out again, closed the doors behind him. Alma, at his prearranged signal, called in to him at the top of her lungs, 'Hurry up, Bill. We'll miss that train!' For the benefit of the two in the kitchen. He got into the car with her and they drove away.

"That was all he did. Brought the gun out of the closet, stepped in here with it, laid it down on a ready-made plotted square on this table, centered at his sleeping brother. He certainly didn't fire it. But that, gentlemen, was the murder of Harry Diedrich, of which I was accused.

"You can take out your watches and time it, if you care to. Or just stand quietly a few minutes and wait for it to happen."

One of them did the former; Ames watched.

It was crawling slowly along the transverse, but too slowly for the eye to detect motion in it.

Once Ames said, perhaps to break the tension of waiting, "How could they be sure of picking up this Struthers, from the next estate down the road, so they'd have an outside, corroboratory witness?"

Townsend shrugged. "Hard to know. But I'd take a guess at it. Maybe she did a little quiet checking up in the morning to find out what neighbor was planning to go to town."

It had hit the exposed powder magazine of the gun now. It lay across it, like a vivid yellow leaf, luminous where all else was cool blue shade.

Minutes slowly went by. You couldn't see it move, but it was moving all the time. You could tell that only in relation to the things around it.

It was starting to slip off the magazine again, on the opposite side.

They watched in silent intensity. Once or twice a face would turn to Townsend, questioningly, then back again without saying anything.

A querulous thread of black unraveled from the open magazine; then freed itself, broke off short, went up into nothingness. No more followed.

Three of the diamond's points were past it now, on the other side of the tiling surface. The fourth still lingered across it, but was retreating fast.

"I get what you were trying to show us," Ames said at last, "but it looks like this time it's not going to pay aw—"

There was a malignant little flash, that made them all jump. Then a jet of red orange shot out the opposite end of the barrel, an angry roar rattled the tiled stand and the panes around on three sides of the enclosure, and a great broil of acrid, sickening smoke huffed out.

Only the base of the lamp remained, nestled in the lower inside corner of the settee. The dome, the bulbs, the supporting stem, had been shorn off clean.

"That," Townsend said, "was Harry Diedrich's head."

"So that's how it was," Ames said,

"That's how it was," Townsend concurred.

"Could be," Ames said. "But don't forget that one honest witness saw you running out of that room with the gun in your hand."

"Lucky for me the old man saw that too," Townsend said. "I was asleep in the room next door. The shot woke me up and I ran in to see what had happened. Evidently I picked up the gun and ran out of the house holding it in my hand. I must have seen the car driving up. I was shouting with excitement." Townsend shrugged. "Naturally they played that for all it was worth. It was a cinch for them to convince Mr. Struthers, who'd been brought back just to be convinced, that I was running out with the gun in my hand to kill them too. Alma probably let out a couple of good loud screams so that Struthers couldn't hear what I was shouting."

"Nice set up," Ames said. There was a sort of grudging respect in his voice.

They filed out of the house and got into the car. The cop on sentinel duty shifted over closer beside the chair out front, put his hand tentatively on the back of it. You could tell he was going to relapse into it as soon as they'd cleared out.

The Diedrich house irised out behind them like something that had never been. Trees got in the way, and it was gone. Somebody looked back. It wasn't Townsend.

"Where do I stand now?" he asked presently.

Ames fingered the edges of the brief case holding an official transcription of Emil Diedrich's optical telegrams. "I'm turning this account of his in to the public prosecutor's office, and of course I'm making out my own report, which'll include what you just showed us. Technically, it won't be in my hands any more from that point on. But—" He gave Townsend an encouraging look. "I don't think you've got much to worry about. They'll put you through the formality of having the murder charges against you dismissed, and then you'll probably be remanded into my custody as a material witness against Harry Diedrich's widow. It won't be much different from being on probation, having to stick around for a certain length of time until the trial's over with. I'll do what I can to make it easy on you."

He began forthwith, as soon as they had reached the constabulary, which formed part of the same building as the jail. "The prisoner's having his meal with me, out here in my office," he informed the guard. "I'll send him back to you later."

He had their dinners sent in from the restaurant across the square, ordered a couple of bottles of beer to be sent with it.

"Gee this must feel funny to you," Townsend said, "sitting here having a quiet meal with me of all people, the guy you were trying so long to get."

"Yeah," Ames admitted. He finished the beer in his glass. "Let's let it go at this. I was after a guy named Dan Nearing. I lost him someplace along the way, between here and Tillary Street. I don't think he'll ever show up again—there or anywhere else." He grinned.

Townsend saw that the gray eyes were friendly.

24

THE TRAIN was coming in. The train back to the present. Back to Virginia. You could hear its hiss and rumble up the yards. It took a slight turn outward, then straightened out again and fanned by, only stopping after you had given up hope and thought it was going to miss New Jericho entirely.

Ames, and the man who was now merely a material witness in the forthcoming case against Alma Diedrich, and the deputy who was to accompany the material witness, had to chase up the platform to keep abreast of it.

The deputy swung aboard first. Townsend put his foot on the bottommost step, swung around to say good-by to Ames.

The latter poked a finger of reminder into his arm, in the same place where he'd once been vaccinated as a kid. "No later than Wednesday now, that was all I could get you. Did you let her know you were coming?"

"No, I'm going to walk in on her from nowhere—like I did once before. Only this time it's for keeps. I'd like to bring her back with me, only I hate to get her mixed up in all the publicity there'll be once the trial opens up."

"I'll take care of that," Ames promised. "I'll get her a room in my boarding house."

The train started to move again. Townsend preceded the deputy into the car, sat down by the window. He slung his hat up on the rack and leaned back. New Jericho was starting to slip backwards. Suddenly he caught sight of something out of the corner of his eye that made him shy away, as in memory of past danger.

Ames was running along opposite the window, on the platform outside, laughing at him with something that flashed metallically.

Townsend threw up the window and Ames thrust in at him the same cigarette case that he had once tried to pawn down on Tillary Street. "You left this in the office last night and I forgot to give it back to you— What're you laughing at?"

"I dunno, life is like a circle, isn't it? We end up like we began. The first time I ever saw you, you were pacing me like that outside a moving window, trying to get in at me."

Ames fell behind, was suddenly whisked up and snatched from sight as the train began to gain its stride. It was not yet at full speed as it shrieked past the sprawling, moss-grown cemetery just outside the village.

Townsend caught a fleeting glimpse of a familiar mound. He saw the small headstone that had been his only gift to Ruth Dillon. Ruth who had given him so much, the past and the future. He raised two fingers to his temple, brought them out again in salute. Salute and farewell.

The locomotive up ahead gave a long, wailing whistle of unutterable sadness. It died away, but it hummed in Townsend's eardrums a second or two longer, like a playback. Then that went too. And with it, he knew, was gone more than the echo of a lonely train whistle over the countryside.

With it, the past was gone.

Forever.

THE END

DISCUSSION QUESTIONS

- Did any aspects of the plot date the story? If so, which?

- Would the story be different if it were set in the present day? If so, how?

- Did the social context of the time play a role in the narrative? If so, how?

- If you were one of the main characters, would you have acted differently at any point in the story?

- Did you identify with any of the characters? If so, which?

- Did this book remind you of any present day authors? If so, which?

- Cornell Woolrich inspired more film noir adaptations than any other author of his time. Why do you think that might be?

OTTO PENZLER PRESENTS
═══AMERICAN MYSTERY CLASSICS═══

All titles are available in hardcover and in trade paperback.

Order from your favorite bookstore or from
The Mysterious Bookshop, 58 Warren Street, New York, N.Y. 10007
(www.mysteriousbookshop.com).

Charlotte Armstrong, *The Chocolate Cobweb*. When Amanda Garth was born, a mix-up caused the hospital to briefly hand her over to the prestigious Garrison family instead of to her birth parents. The error was quickly fixed, Amanda was never told, and the secret was forgotten for twenty-three years … until her aunt revealed it in casual conversation. But what if the initial switch never actually occurred? **Introduction by A. J. Finn.**

Charlotte Armstrong, *The Unsuspected*. First published in 1946, this suspenseful novel opens with a young woman who has ostensibly hanged herself, leaving a suicide note. Her friend doesn't believe it and begins an investigation that puts her own life in jeopardy. It was filmed in 1947 by Warner Brothers, starring Claude Rains and Joan Caulfield. **Introduction by Otto Penzler.**

Anthony Boucher, *The Case of the Baker Street Irregulars*. When a studio announces a new hard-boiled Sherlock Holmes film, the Baker Street Irregulars begin a campaign to discredit it. Attempting to mollify them, the producers invite members to the set, where threats are received, each referring to one of the original Holmes tales, followed by murder. Fortunately, the amateur sleuths use Holmesian lessons to solve the crime. **Introduction by Otto Penzler.**

Anthony Boucher, *Rocket to the Morgue*. Hilary Foulkes has made so many enemies that it is difficult to speculate who was responsible for stabbing him nearly to death in a room with only one door through which no one was seen entering or leaving. This classic locked room mystery is populated by such thinly disguised science fiction legends as Robert Heinlein, L. Ron Hubbard, and John W. Campbell. **Introduction by F. Paul Wilson.**

Fredric Brown, *The Fabulous Clipjoint*. Brown's outstanding mystery won an Edgar as the best first novel of the year (1947). When Wallace

Hunter is found dead in an alley after a long night of drinking, the police don't really care. But his teenage son Ed and his uncle Am, the carnival worker, are convinced that some things don't add up and the crime isn't what it seems to be. **Introduction by Lawrence Block.**

John Dickson Carr, *The Crooked Hinge*. Selected by a group of mystery experts as one of the 15 best impossible crime novels ever written, this is one of Gideon Fell's greatest challenges. Estranged from his family for 25 years, Sir John Farnleigh returns to England from America to claim his inheritance but another person turns up claiming that he can prove he is the real Sir John. Inevitably, one of them is murdered. **Introduction by Charles Todd.**

John Dickson Carr, *The Eight of Swords*. When Gideon Fell arrives at a crime scene, it appears to be straightforward enough. A man has been shot to death in an unlocked room and the likely perpetrator was a recent visitor. But Fell discovers inconsistencies and his investigations are complicated by an apparent poltergeist, some American gangsters, and two meddling amateur sleuths. **Introduction by Otto Penzler.**

John Dickson Carr, *The Mad Hatter Mystery*. A prankster has been stealing top hats all around London. Gideon Fell suspects that the same person may be responsible for the theft of a manuscript of a long-lost story by Edgar Allan Poe. The hats reappear in unexpected but conspicuous places but, when one is found on the head of a corpse by the Tower of London, it is evident that the thefts are more than pranks. **Introduction by Otto Penzler.**

John Dickson Carr, *The Plague Court Murders*. When murder occurs in a locked hut on Plague Court, an estate haunted by the ghost of a hangman's assistant who died a victim of the black death, Sir Henry Merrivale seeks a logical solution to a ghostly crime. A spiritual medium employed to rid the house of his spirit is found stabbed to death in a locked stone hut on the grounds, surrounded by an untouched circle of mud. **Introduction by Michael Dirda.**

John Dickson Carr, *The Red Widow Murders.* In a "haunted" mansion, the room known as the Red Widow's Chamber proves lethal to all who spend the night. Eight people investigate and the one who draws the ace of spades must sleep in it. The room is locked from the inside and watched all night by the others. When the door is unlocked, the victim has been poisoned. Enter Sir Henry Merrivale to solve the crime. **Introduction by Tom Mead.**

Frances Crane, *The Turquoise Shop.* In an arty little New Mexico town, Mona Brandon has arrived from the East and becomes the subject of gossip about her money, her influence, and the corpse in the nearby desert who may be her husband. Pat Holly, who runs the local gift shop, is as interested as anyone in the goings on—but even more in Pat Abbott, the detective investigating the possible murder. **Introduction by Anne Hillerman.**

Todd Downing, *Vultures in the Sky.* There is no end to the series of terrifying events that befall a luxury train bound for Mexico. First, a man dies when the train passes through a dark tunnel, then it comes to an abrupt stop in the middle of the desert. More deaths occur when night falls and the passengers panic when they realize they are trapped with a murderer on the loose. **Introduction by James Sallis.**

Mignon G. Eberhart, *Murder by an Aristocrat.* Nurse Keate is called to help a man who has been "accidentally" shot in the shoulder. When he is murdered while convalescing, it is clear that there was no accident. Although a killer is loose in the mansion, the family seems more concerned that news of the murder will leave their circle. *The New Yorker* wrote than "Eberhart can weave an almost flawless mystery." **Introduction by Nancy Pickard.**

Erle Stanley Gardner, *The Case of the Baited Hook.* Perry Mason gets a phone call in the middle of the night and his potential client says it's urgent, that he has two one-thousand-dollar bills that he will give him as a retainer, with an additional ten-thousand whenever he is called on to represent him. When Mason takes the case, it is not for the caller but for a beautiful woman whose identity is hidden behind a mask. **Introduction by Otto Penzler.**

Erle Stanley Gardner, *The Case of the Borrowed Brunette.* A mysterious man named Mr. Hines has advertised a job for a woman who has to fulfill very specific physical requirements. Eva Martell, pretty but struggling in her career as a model, takes the job but her aunt smells a rat and hires Perry Mason to investigate. Her fears are realized when Hines turns up in the apartment with a bullet hole in his head. **Introduction by Otto Penzler.**

Erle Stanley Gardner, *The Case of the Careless Kitten.* Helen Kendal receives a mysterious phone call from her vanished uncle Franklin, long presumed dead, who urges her to contact Perry Mason. Soon, she finds herself the main suspect in the murder of an unfamiliar man. Her kitten has just survived a poisoning attempt—as has her aunt Matilda. What is the connection between Franklin's return and the murder attempts? **Introduction by Otto Penzler.**

Erle Stanley Gardner, *The Case of the Rolling Bones.* One of Gardner's most successful Perry Mason novels opens with a clear case of blackmail, though the person being blackmailed claims he isn't. It is not long before the police are searching for someone wanted for killing the same man in two different states—thirty-three years apart. The confounding puzzle of what happened to the dead man's toes is a challenge. **Introduction by Otto Penzler.**

Erle Stanley Gardner, *The Case of the Shoplifter's Shoe.* Most cases for Perry Mason involve murder but here he is hired because a young woman fears her aunt is a kleptomaniac. Sarah may not have been precisely the best guardian for a collection of valuable diamonds and, sure enough, they go missing. When the jeweler is found shot dead, Sarah is spotted leaving the murder scene with a bundle of gems stuffed in her purse. **Introduction by Otto Penzler.**

Erle Stanley Gardner, *The Bigger They Come.* Gardner's first novel using the pseudonym A.A. Fair starts off a series featuring the large and loud Bertha Cool and her employee, the small and meek Donald Lam. Given the job of delivering divorce papers to an evident crook,

Lam can't find him—but neither can the police. The *Los Angeles Times* called this book: "Breathlessly dramatic … an original." Introduction by Otto Penzler.

Frances Noyes Hart, *The Bellamy Trial*. Inspired by the real-life Hall-Mills case, the most sensational trial of its day, this is the story of Stephen Bellamy and Susan Ives, accused of murdering Bellamy's wife Madeleine. Eight days of dynamic testimony, some true, some not, make headlines for an enthralled public. Rex Stout called this historic courtroom thriller one of the ten best mysteries of all time. Introduction by Hank Phillippi Ryan.

H.F. Heard, *A Taste for Honey*. The elderly Mr. Mycroft quietly keeps bees in Sussex, where he is approached by the reclusive and somewhat misanthropic Mr. Silchester, whose honey supplier was found dead, stung to death by her bees. Mycroft, who shares many traits with Sherlock Holmes, sets out to find the vicious killer. Rex Stout described it as "sinister … a tale well and truly told." Introduction by Otto Penzler.

Dolores Hitchens, *The Alarm of the Black Cat*. Detective fiction aficionado Rachel Murdock has a peculiar meeting with a little girl and a dead toad, sparking her curiosity about a love triangle that has sparked anger. When the girl's great grandmother is found dead, Rachel and her cat Samantha work with a friend in the Los Angeles Police Department to get to the bottom of things. Introduction by David Handler.

Dolores Hitchens, *The Cat Saw Murder*. Miss Rachel Murdock, the highly intelligent 70-year-old amateur sleuth, is not entirely heartbroken when her slovenly, unattractive, bridge-cheating niece is murdered. Miss Rachel is happy to help the socially maladroit and somewhat bumbling Detective Lieutenant Stephen Mayhew, retaining her composure when a second brutal murder occurs. Introduction by Joyce Carol Oates.

Dorothy B. Hughes, *Dread Journey*. A bigshot Hollywood producer has worked on his magnum opus for years, hiring and firing one beautiful starlet after another. But Kitten Agnew's contract won't allow her to be fired, so she fears she might be terminated more permanently. Together with the producer on a train journey from Hollywood to Chicago, Kitten becomes more terrified with each passing mile. Introduction by Sarah Weinman.

Dorothy B. Hughes, *Ride the Pink Horse*. When Sailor met Willis Douglass, he was just a poor kid who Douglass groomed to work as a confidential secretary. As the senator became increasingly corrupt, he knew he could count on Sailor to clean up his messes. No longer a senator, Douglass flees Chicago for Santa Fe, leaving behind a murder rap and Sailor as the prime suspect. Seeking vengeance, Sailor follows. Introduction by Sara Paretsky.

Dorothy B. Hughes, *The So Blue Marble*. Set in the glamorous world of New York high society, this novel became a suspense classic as twins from Europe try to steal a rare and beautiful gem owned by an aristocrat whose sister is an even more menacing presence. *The New Yorker* called it "Extraordinary … [Hughes'] brilliant descriptive powers make and unmake reality." Introduction by Otto Penzler.

W. Bolingbroke Johnson, *The Widening Stain*. After a cocktail party, the attractive Lucie Coindreau, a "black-eyed, black-haired Frenchwoman" visits the rare books wing of the library and apparently takes a headfirst fall from an upper gallery. Dismissed as a horrible accident, it seems dubious when Professor Hyett is strangled while reading a priceless 12th-century manuscript, which has gone missing. Introduction by Nicholas A. Basbanes

Baynard Kendrick, *Blind Man's Bluff*. Blinded in World War II, Duncan Maclain forms a successful private detective agency, aided by his two dogs. Here, he is called on to solve the case of a blind man who plummets from the top of an eight-story building, apparently with no one present except his dead-drunk son. Introduction by Otto Penzler.

Baynard Kendrick, *The Odor of Violets*. Duncan Maclain, a blind former intelligence officer, is asked to investigate the murder of an actor in his Greenwich Village apartment. This would cause a stir at any time but, when the actor possesses secret government plans that then go missing, it's enough to interest the local police as well as the American government and Maclain, who suspects a German spy plot. Introduction by Otto Penzler.

C. Daly King, *Obelists at Sea*. On a cruise ship traveling from New York to Paris, the lights of the smoking room briefly go out, a gunshot crashes through the night, and a man is dead. Two detectives are on board but so are four psychiatrists who believe their professional knowledge can solve the case by understanding the psyche of the killer—each with a different theory. **Introduction by Martin Edwards.**

Jonathan Latimer, *Headed for a Hearse*. Featuring Bill Crane, the booze-soaked Chicago private detective, this humorous hard-boiled novel was filmed as *The Westland Case* in 1937 starring Preston Foster. Robert Westland has been framed for the grisly murder of his wife in a room with doors and windows locked from the inside. As the day of his execution nears, he relies on Crane to find the real murderer. **Introduction by Max Allan Collins**

Lange Lewis, *The Birthday Murder*. Victoria is a successful novelist and screenwriter and her husband is a movie director so their marriage seems almost too good to be true. Then, on her birthday, her happy new life comes crashing down when her husband is murdered using a method of poisoning that was described in one of her books. She quickly becomes the leading suspect. **Introduction by Randal S. Brandt.**

Frances and Richard Lockridge, *Death on the Aisle*. In one of the most beloved books to feature Mr. and Mrs. North, the body of a wealthy backer of a play is found dead in a seat of the 45th Street Theater. Pam is thrilled to engage in her favorite pastime—playing amateur sleuth—much to the annoyance of Jerry, her publisher husband. The Norths inspired a stage play, a film, and long-running radio and TV series. **Introduction by Otto Penzler.**

John P. Marquand, *Your Turn, Mr. Moto*. The first novel about Mr. Moto, originally titled *No Hero*, is the story of a World War I hero pilot who finds himself jobless during the Depression. In Tokyo for a big opportunity that falls apart, he meets a Japanese agent and his Russian colleague and the pilot suddenly finds himself caught in a web of intrigue. Peter Lorre played Mr. Moto in a series of popular films. **Introduction by Lawrence Block.**

Stuart Palmer, *The Penguin Pool Murder*. The first adventure of schoolteacher and dedicated amateur sleuth Hildegarde Withers occurs at the New York Aquarium when she and her young students notice a corpse in one of the tanks. It was published in 1931 and filmed the next year, starring Edna May Oliver as the American Miss Marple—though much funnier than her English counterpart. **Introduction by Otto Penzler.**

Stuart Palmer, *The Puzzle of the Happy Hooligan*. New York City schoolteacher Hildegarde Withers cannot resist "assisting" homicide detective Oliver Piper. In this novel, she is on vacation in Hollywood and on the set of a movie about Lizzie Borden when the screenwriter is found dead. Six comic films about Withers appeared in the 1930s, most successfully starring Edna May Oliver. **Introduction by Otto Penzler.**

Otto Penzler, ed., *Golden Age Bibliomysteries*. Stories of murder, theft, and suspense occur with alarming regularity in the unlikely world of books and bibliophiles, including bookshops, libraries, and private rare book collections, written by such giants of the mystery genre as Ellery Queen, Cornell Woolrich, Lawrence G. Blochman, Vincent Starrett, and Anthony Boucher. **Introduction by Otto Penzler.**

Otto Penzler, ed., *Golden Age Detective Stories*. The history of American mystery fiction has its pantheon of authors who have influenced and entertained readers for nearly a century, reaching its peak during the Golden Age, and this collection pays homage to the work of the most acclaimed: Cornell Woolrich, Erle Stanley Gardner, Craig Rice, Ellery Queen, Dorothy B. Hughes, Mary Roberts Rinehart, and more. **Introduction by Otto Penzler.**

Otto Penzler, ed., *Golden Age Locked Room Mysteries*. The so-called impossible crime category reached its zenith during the 1920s, 1930s, and 1940s, and this volume includes the greatest of the great authors who mastered the form: John Dickson Carr, Ellery Queen, C. Daly King, Clayton Rawson, and Erle Stanley Gardner. Like great magicians, these literary conjurors will baffle and delight readers. **Introduction by Otto Penzler.**

Ellery Queen, *The Adventures of Ellery Queen*. These stories are the earliest short works to feature Queen as a detective and are among the best of the author's fair-play mysteries. So many of the elements that comprise the gestalt of Queen may be found in these tales: alternate solutions, the dying clue, a bizarre crime, and the author's ability to find fresh variations of works by other authors. **Introduction by Otto Penzler.**

Ellery Queen, *The American Gun Mystery*. A rodeo comes to New York City at the Colosseum. The headliner is Buck Horne, the once popular film cowboy who opens the show leading a charge of forty whooping cowboys until they pull out their guns and fire into the air. Buck falls to the ground, shot dead. The police instantly lock the doors to search everyone but the offending weapon has completely vanished. **Introduction by Otto Penzler.**

Ellery Queen, *The Chinese Orange Mystery*. The offices of publisher Donald Kirk have seen strange events but nothing like this. A strange man is found dead with two long spears alongside his back. And, though no one was seen entering or leaving the room, everything has been turned backwards or upside down: pictures face the wall, the victim's clothes are worn backwards, the rug upside down. Why in the world? **Introduction by Otto Penzler.**

Ellery Queen, *The Dutch Shoe Mystery*. Millionaire philanthropist Abagail Doorn falls into a coma and she is rushed to the hospital she funds for an emergency operation by one of the leading surgeons on the East Coast. When she is wheeled into the operating theater, the sheet covering her body is pulled back to reveal her garroted corpse—the first of a series of murders **Introduction by Otto Penzler.**

Ellery Queen, *The Egyptian Cross Mystery*. A small-town schoolteacher is found dead, headed, and tied to a T-shaped cross on December 25th, inspiring such sensational headlines as "Crucifixion on Christmas Day." Amateur sleuth Ellery Queen is so intrigued he travels to Virginia but fails to solve the crime. Then a similar murder takes place on New York's Long Island—and then another. **Introduction by Otto Penzler.**

Ellery Queen, *The Siamese Twin Mystery*. When Ellery and his father encounter a raging forest fire on a mountain, their only hope is to drive up to an isolated hillside manor owned by a secretive surgeon and his strange guests. While playing solitaire in the middle of the night, the doctor is shot. The only clue is a torn playing card. Suspects include a society beauty, a valet, and conjoined twins. **Introduction by Otto Penzler.**

Ellery Queen, *The Spanish Cape Mystery*. Amateur detective Ellery Queen arrives in the resort town of Spanish Cape soon after a young woman and her uncle are abducted by a gun-toting, one-eyed giant. The next day, the woman's somewhat dicey boyfriend is found murdered—totally naked under a black fedora and opera cloak. **Introduction by Otto Penzler.**

Patrick Quentin, *A Puzzle for Fools*. Broadway producer Peter Duluth takes to the bottle when his wife dies but enters a sanitarium to dry out. Malevolent events plague the hospital, including when Peter hears his own voice intone, "There will be murder." And there is. He investigates, aided by a young woman who is also a patient. This is the first of nine mysteries featuring Peter and Iris Duluth. **Introduction by Otto Penzler.**

Clayton Rawson, *Death from a Top Hat*. When the New York City Police Department is baffled by an apparently impossible crime, they call on The Great Merlini, a retired stage magician who now runs a Times Square magic shop. In his first case, two occultists have been murdered in a room locked from the inside, their bodies positioned to form a pentagram. **Introduction by Otto Penzler.**

Craig Rice, *Eight Faces at Three*. Gin-soaked John J. Malone, defender of the guilty, is notorious for getting his culpable clients off. It's the innocent ones who are problems. Like Holly Inglehart, accused of piercing the black heart of her well-heeled aunt Alexandria with a lovely Florentine paper cutter. No one who knew the old battle-ax liked her, but Holly's prints were found on the murder weapon. **Introduction by Lisa Lutz.**

Craig Rice, *Home Sweet Homicide*. Known as the Dorothy Parker of mystery fiction for her memorable wit, Craig Rice was the first detective writer to appear on the cover of *Time* magazine. This comic mystery features two kids who are trying to find a husband for their widowed mother while she's engaged in sleuthing. Filmed with the same title in 1946 with Peggy Ann Garner and Randolph Scott. Introduction by Otto Penzler.

Mary Roberts Rinehart, *The Album*. Crescent Place is a quiet enclave of wealthy people in which nothing ever happens—until a bedridden old woman is attacked by an intruder with an ax. *The New York Times* stated: "All Mary Roberts Rinehart mystery stories are good, but this one is better." Introduction by Otto Penzler.

Mary Roberts Rinehart, *The Haunted Lady*. The arsenic in her sugar bowl was wealthy widow Eliza Fairbanks' first clue that somebody wanted her dead. Nightly visits of bats, birds, and rats, obviously aimed at scaring the dowager to death, was the second. Eliza calls the police, who send nurse Hilda Adams, the amateur sleuth they refer to as "Miss Pinkerton," to work undercover to discover the culprit. Introduction by Otto Penzler.

Mary Roberts Rinehart, *Miss Pinkerton*. Hilda Adams is a nurse, not a detective, but she is observant and smart and so it is common for Inspector Patton to call on her for help. Her success results in his calling her "Miss Pinkerton." *The New Republic* wrote: "From thousands of hearts and homes the cry will go up: Thank God for Mary Roberts Rinehart." Introduction by Carolyn Hart.

Mary Roberts Rinehart, *The Red Lamp*. Professor William Porter refuses to believe that the seaside manor he's just inherited is haunted but he has to convince his wife to move in. However, he soon sees evidence of the occult phenomena of which the townspeople speak. Whether it is a spirit or a human being, Porter accepts that there is a connection to the rash of murders that have terrorized the countryside. Introduction by Otto Penzler.

Mary Roberts Rinehart, *The Wall*. For two decades, Mary Roberts Rinehart was the second-best-selling author in America (only Sinclair Lewis outsold her) and was beloved for her tales of suspense. In a magnificent mansion, the ex-wife of one of the owners turns up making demands and is found dead the next day. And there are more dark secrets lying behind the walls of the estate. Introduction by Otto Penzler.

Joel Townsley Rogers, *The Red Right Hand*. This extraordinary whodunnit that is as puzzling as it is terrifying was identified by crime fiction scholar Jack Adrian as "one of the dozen or so finest mystery novels of the 20th century." A deranged killer sends a doctor on a quest for the truth—deep into the recesses of his own mind—when he and his bride-to-be elope but pick up a terrifying sharp-toothed hitch-hiker. Introduction by Joe R. Lansdale.

Roger Scarlett, *Cat's Paw*. The family of the wealthy old bachelor Martin Greenough cares far more about his money than they do about him. For his birthday, he invites all his potential heirs to his mansion to tell them what they hope to hear. Before he can disburse funds, however, he is murdered, and the Boston Police Department's big problem is that there are too many suspects. Introduction by Curtis Evans

Vincent Starrett, *Dead Man Inside*. 1930s Chicago is a tough town but some crimes are more bizarre than others. Customers arrive at a haberdasher to find a corpse in the window and a sign on the door: *Dead Man Inside! I am Dead. The store will not open today.* This is just one of a series of odd murders that terrorizes the city. Reluctant detective Walter Ghost leaps into action to learn what is behind the plague. Introduction by Otto Penzler.

Vincent Starrett, *The Great Hotel Murder*. Theater critic and amateur sleuth Riley Blackwood investigates a murder in a Chicago hotel where the dead man had changed rooms with a stranger who had registered under a fake name. *The New York Times* described it as "an ingenious plot with enough complications to keep the reader guessing." Introduction by Lyndsay Faye.

Vincent Starrett, *Murder on 'B' Deck*. Walter Ghost, a psychologist, scientist, explorer, and former intelligence officer, is on a cruise ship and his friend novelist Dunsten Mollock, a Nigel Bruce-like Watson whose role is to offer occasional comic relief, accommodates when he fails to leave the ship before it takes off. Although they make mistakes along the way, the amateur sleuths solve the shipboard murders. Introduction by Ray Betzner.

Phoebe Atwood Taylor, *The Cape Cod Mystery*. Vacationers have flocked to Cape Cod to avoid the heat wave that hit the Northeast and find their holiday unpleasant when the area is flooded with police trying to find the murderer of a muckraking journalist who took a cottage for the season. Finding a solution falls to Asey Mayo, "the Cape Cod Sherlock," known for his worldly wisdom, folksy humor, and common sense. **Introduction by Otto Penzler.**

S. S. Van Dine, *The Benson Murder Case.* The first of 12 novels to feature Philo Vance, the most popular and influential detective character of the early part of the 20th century. When wealthy stockbroker Alvin Benson is found shot to death in a locked room in his mansion, the police are baffled until the erudite flaneur and art collector arrives on the scene. Paramount filmed it in 1930 with William Powell as Vance. **Introduction by Ragnar Jónasson.**

Cornell Woolrich, *The Bride Wore Black.* The first suspense novel by one of the greatest of all noir authors opens with a bride and her new husband walking out of the church. A car speeds by, shots ring out, and he falls dead at her feet. Determined to avenge his death, she tracks down everyone in the car, concluding with a shocking surprise. It was filmed by Francois Truffaut in 1968, starring Jeanne Moreau. **Introduction by Eddie Muller.**

Cornell Woolrich, *Deadline at Dawn.* Quinn is overcome with guilt about having robbed a stranger's home. He meets Bricky, a dime-a-dance girl, and they fall for each other. When they return to the crime scene, they discover a dead body. Knowing Quinn will be accused of the crime, they race to find the true killer before he's arrested. A 1946 film starring Susan Hayward was loosely based on the plot. **Introduction by David Gordon.**

Cornell Woolrich, *Waltz into Darkness.* A New Orleans businessman successfully courts a woman through the mail but he is shocked to find when she arrives that she is not the plain brunette whose picture he'd received but a radiant blond beauty. She soon absconds with his fortune. Wracked with disappointment and loneliness, he vows to track her down. When he finds her, the real nightmare begins. **Introduction by Wallace Stroby.**